THREE MYSTERIES BY
JOHNSTON McCULLEY

THREE MYSTERIES BY JOHNSTON McCULLEY

Johnston McCulley

WILDSIDE PRESS

THREE MYSTERIES BY JOHNSTON McCULLEY

All stories originally appeared in *Detective Story Magazine.*

CONTENTS

A CROOK WITHOUT HONOR

HIS lips curled in a sneer, his little eyes glittering, Jim Morlan stood against the bole of the tree in the darkness and watched the patrolman go slowly along the walk, swinging his stick, his helmet on the back of his head, sniffing at the roses that grew along the edge of the lawn, looking up at the big moon, enjoying the perfect summer night.

"Ass!" Jim Morlan growled to himself.

It was the habit of Jim Morlan to regard almost everybody in that light. To him, all other human beings were inferiors. It was a state of mind he had acquired in boyhood, and it had grown with his great body until it had taken full possession of him and molded his character. It had cost him all his friends and a great majority of his mere acquaintances. Jim Morlan, in that particular corner of the underworld, stood alone. He was known as a crooked crook. He did not possess even the questionable honor of his profession. Openly, he said that he would as soon rob another crook as an honest man. The "honor among thieves" idea he called "bunk."

The unsuspecting patrolman, possibly thinking of his cottage, his wife, and his children, passed on down the street and finally turned a corner. Jim Morlan knew, because he had made it his business to know, that he would not return to this vicinity for more than an hour. This was the select residence portion of the city, and the patrolman had a big beat. There were a few private watchmen scattered around, but Jim Morlan knew them and their habits and had nothing to fear from them.

Yet he hesitated for a moment to be sure, and then he crept like a shadow into another shadow cast by a clump of shrubs, and from that to still another made by a big tree, and in this manner he worked his way from the street to the side of the big house he intended to rob.

Morlan knew all about that house, too. He knew that the family had gone to the mountains for a month, that the master of the house spent a part of the time in town, that there were but three servants in the place, and that they slept on the third floor in the rear. They were no more than caretakers. The better servants had been sent to the mountain lodge with the family. Morlan had nothing to fear from the three who remained.

In the library of that residence, there was a safe hidden behind a panel in the wall. Jim Morlan knew that it contained some old jewelry that never was used, but which would bring considerable cash when properly handled by a "fence." He expected to find some ready money, too, for he had ascertained that it was the policy of the master of the house to keep a supply in the safe at all times.

Nor was that all. There was a tray of ancient coins in the safe, so the fence had said, and an unscrupulous collector in another city would pay a big price for a particular coin in the tray. Jim Morlan expected to make a good thing out of this night's work.

And it was necessary, he told himself. He was almost out of funds, thanks to an idea that he could play poker. He knew that the men who had strapped him were exulting, not only because they had taken the money, but also because they had taken it from him.

For Jim Morlan was cordially hated by the others of the underworld. He never played fair. He always worked alone. He did not give loyalty to his kind, and expected none. He belonged to no class, but stood alone. He had gone out of his way some months before to swindle a pair of crooks.

And there was a keen determination throughout the underworld to "get" him. There was no idea of turning him over to the police. The idea was to make him a laughingstock, to kill him with ridicule.

Morlan did not think of these things as he came finally to the side of the big house and crouched in the darkness near the wall. He watched and listened for a time. In the distance, some clock struck the hour of one. The district was quiet. There was scarcely a light to be seen, save here and there a soft glow from a entry hall or servants' quarters.

Morlan slipped along the wall until he came to a basement window. He did not break the catch with a jimmy. He guessed that the window was connected with a burglar-alarm system. Putting a rubber suction cap in the middle of the glass, he held it there with his left hand and, with his right, cut out the window close to the sash, using a glass cutter of the most approved pattern.

A quick pull, a snap, and the pane of glass came away with scarcely any noise. Jim Morlan crawled through and found himself in a laundry room.

Now he flashed his electric torch and found a piece of carpet, which he stretched before the open window. None knew better than Morlan that a sudden gust of wind might come through that window, slam a door somewhere in the house, and awaken the servants.

The window covered, Morlan flashed his electric torch again and made his way into a hall. Finding a flight of steps, he crept upwards and presently found himself on the ground floor of the house. He stopped for a moment to watch and listen, the torch extinguished. Then he padded through the hall toward the library.

Once inside the library, with the hall door closed behind him, Morlan felt his way around the walls until he had drawn all the window shades tightly. Only then did he flash the torch again. He did not want a sudden flash of light to go outside, possibly to be seen by some passing watchman and arouse curiosity.

He knew where the safe was located and how to slide back the panel in the wall, and he lost no time in doing so. And then he knelt before the safe and played the light of the torch on the combination knob.

Jim Morlan always was well prepared when he turned a trick. He knew a great deal about this particular safe. It was an imposing thing, but as a matter of truth, it presented no great difficulties to a finished cracksman. What it had in appearance it lacked in security.

He worked at the combination slowly, his ear pressed close to the steel dial. He made a mistake once, growled low down in his throat, and began anew. And finally he triumphed and, with a grunt of satisfaction, swung the heavy door of the safe open.

Now his torch was extinguished again for a moment, while, holding his breath, Jim Morlan listened again. He heard not the slightest sound to indicate the presence of danger. Satisfied that everything was as it should be, he once more flashed the torch.

The strong box was before him. Morlan took a tool from the lining of his coat and snapped the lock. He pulled the strong box out. Jewels flashed in the light, gems in old-fashioned settings that made Morlan's eyes glitter with avarice.

Morlan extracted them and put them in a pile on the carpet before him. He opened another drawer and found a package of currency—a couple of hundred dollars, he guessed. It was not so much as he had expected, but it came in handy. And now he would have to find the tray of old coins.

It did not take him long to find them. Putting the tray on the bottom of the safe, he glanced over it rapidly, seeking the particular coin he had been told to get. He wanted to put that in a special pocket, away from the others. It was to be the best part of the night's haul.

A sound reached his ears. Morlan snapped out the torch and remained silent and motionless, crouching before the safe. He heard the sound again—steps in the hall.

A door creaked as though it was being opened slowly. Morlan took a revolver from his pocket and held it ready. He was caught, in a way, if this unknown entered the library and snapped on the lights. But he would have the advantage of surprise, perhaps—and he could make a get-away. He did not have time to scoop up the coins and the jewelry and currency and slip the loot into one of his pockets. He heard the rustling of silk. And then the lights flashed on.

Just inside the hall door stood a young woman in evening dress.

CHAPTER II

Jim Morlan sprang to his feet and menaced her with the revolver.

"Oh!" she gasped.

"Silence!" Morlan commanded. "Shut that door behind you! Not a sound or I'll shoot!"

She seemed stupefied, but she obeyed mechanically, as though through the force of the fear he had inspired. She closed the door gently, and then swayed against the wall, one hand to her forehead.

"Sit down over there by that table!" Morlan commanded in a hoarse whisper.

She staggered across the room and collapsed in the chair. Her eyes were wide, and she appeared to be badly frightened.

"You—you're a burglar!" she whispered. "You—you were robbing the safe—'"

"Naw, I'm just the rent collector," Morlan whispered in reply, grinning. "Seems to me you butted in at the wrong time. What're you doin' here? I understood the family was in the mountains."

"You—robbing the safe—"

"Yeh, I suppose so. You just be quiet now and don't make a move, and as soon as I collect these little trophies I've found I'll decide what to do with you. I can't be havin' my get-away spoiled by any young skirt."

She seemed to be breathing easier now. She bent forward a bit in her chair. Morlan glanced sharply at her and stooped to pick up the swag.

"Wait!" she implored. "I—I don't belong in this house—"

"Then what are you doin' here?" Morlan asked. "Burglar yourself?"

"I—yes, in a way."

"That's good! You don't look the part," said Morlan. "Folks don't burgle in Paris gowns and with their hair dressed that way. Are you tryin' to play some kind of a game on me? Anybody else comin' after you?"

"No."

"You play a trick, my lady, and it'll be your last. This gun I'm holdin' is a businesslike little article."

"I—please listen to me," she begged. "Maybe you—can help me—"

"I don't quite get this."

"Listen," she begged again. "I—I came here—to get something, I had a key to the front door. I don't belong in this house, but I—I've been a guest here often. I belong to the same social set—"

"What's all this?" Morlan wanted to know.

"Do you know whose house this is?" she asked.

"Sure. It's Blakeley's house."

"And do you know Blakeley? A polished gentleman, isn't he—rich, has social position, charitable, all that!"

She sneered. "Do you know why I am here?" she asked.

"I'm listenin'."

"Blakeley is a man of fifty-five, a widower."

"I know all that. Get down to cases."

"And he—he wants to marry me. Can you imagine me marrying a man like him? There—there is another man, you see, but that doesn't stop Blakeley. And so—"

"Pardon me, lady, but I ain't got time to hear the latest society news."

"Please wait—listen, and help me. I'll make it worth your while. See—see these rings? They are worth several thousand, I suppose. I—I'll give them to you if you'll help me!"

"Very nice. But I can just take 'em without helpin' you at all," said Morlan.

"But you wouldn't do that, I'm sure. And it is such a little thing I want."

"Go ahead with the story."

"I've got a foolish young brother. Blakeley got him gambling at the club, and he—he forged a check. And now Blakeley has it—and if I don't agree to marry him—"

"He'll hand the boy over to the cops?"

"Yes," she breathed. "It's an old scheme, of course, but it is terrible for all that. I want to save my brother—and myself. I knew the family was away, and I slipped here from a party. I had some wild idea of getting that check."

"You think it is in the safe?"

"Possibly. Either there or in the desk. Get it for me, and I'll give you these rings. Here—take them now!"

She stripped them from her fingers, and Morlan took them from her hand and stepped back. His eyes glittered as he looked at them. Three or four thousand, at least, he thought. He chuckled as he looked at her again. "Well, I'll play fair for once, lady," he said. "I've already got the safe open, and if the check's here, you can have it."

"And I hope—hope you take everything else!" she whispered. "Blakeley deserves it. But just get me the check and then let me get away. And I'll thank you—and thank you! It is for eight hundred dollars, made payable to Peter van Lyne."

Jim Morlan knelt before the safe and pulled out a bundle of documents, bonds, receipts, lists of securities. Perhaps the check would be there, he thought. He'd give it to the fool girl, then take the other stuff and make his get-away. He would have nothing to fear from her. He might even learn her identity, and there would be possibilities of blackmail in the future.

He began going through the papers. Once he glanced at her, and she had settled back in the chair again and was breathing heavily, evidently listening intently. She was frightened half to death, Morlan decided.

He put his revolver down on the floor and hurried through the papers. He wanted to be done and on his way. He turned his head away from her for an instant—

A sudden swish of silken skirts! Morlan turned quickly. She was out of the chair, standing just before him, her eyes flashing and a terrible look in her face. And she held a wicked-looking automatic that covered him steadily.

"Up with your hands!" she ordered. "Up, or you're a dead man!"

Morlan was caught fairly. The unexpectedness of it did for him as much as the sight of the automatic. He lifted his hands slowly, while his lower jaw sagged in surprise and his eyes bulged.

"Clever little burglar, aren't you?" she said sneeringly. "You swallowed that story neatly, put aside your gun, let me catch you. Not very quick-witted, are you? A few years in prison may improve your wits."

"You—you—" Morlan gasped.

"Walk across the room and sit down in that chair!" she commanded. "And just try a trick, if you think it is best."

Morlan obeyed. He was alert, watching for a chance to make his getaway, but he did not have much hope. Something seemed to tell him that this girl would shoot at the slightest provocation.

"I—was helpin' you—" he stammered.

"You fell for my story, that's all! I got you to put aside your gun, turn away your head—"

"What—you goin' to do?" he asked.

"What does a person generally do when a burglar is caught? You sit still, please."

She reached for the telephone on the table at her elbow. As she took down the receiver she held the automatic in her right hand, and not once did she take her eyes from his.

She called a number. Jim Morlan knew that number well—it was police headquarters!

"Send officers at once to 1720 Norton Place!" she ordered. "I've caught a burglar!"

The receiver was returned to the hook, and once more she settled back in her chair, watching him.

"On your way to prison," she said. "I always had an opinion that professional burglars were clever, but it seems not."

"Let me go," Morlan begged suddenly. "I—everything is there by the safe. I haven't anything in my pockets except your rings. I'll give those back—"

"A man who transgresses the law must pay the penalty," she told him.

"I—I was driven to it," Morlan whimpered. "Give me a chance, lady."

"And you'd be robbing somebody else tomorrow night."

"No! I'll turn straight! If I got to prison now I'll always be a crook. Give me a chance, lady, and I'll turn straight."

"I am afraid not," she said.

She got up from the chair, and, still watching him, moved slowly to the hall door. She turned halfway from him, opened the door, glanced out into the hall, and closed the door again.

"No use to call the servants," she said. "I'll just watch you until the police come."

"For Heaven's sake, lady, let me go!" Jim Morlan implored. "I'll run straight from now on."

"If I could believe that—" she said.

"I swear it, lady,"

"You're frightened now because the police are coming. Tomorrow, over your fright, you'd decide that you had been a fool," she said. "You'd turn burglar again. Prison is the best place for you."

"Ain't you got any mercy?" he asked.

"Mercy isn't extended to criminals," she replied. "You cut yourself off from mercy when you turned crook."

"Just give me a chance! I'll never forget it, lady! And I swear to go straight!"

Jim Morlan thought that he was a consummate actor. He had no more intention of going straight than he had of running for mayor. But he managed real tears and a dry sob or two. And meanwhile he watched her carefully.

It was about time for the police to arrive, he judged. She seemed to think so, too. She got up again and once more moved toward the hall door.

Jim Morlan took the chance. He was out of his chair like a shot and at the nearest window. He crashed through it, darted across the lawn, made for the nearest alley. And as he ran he exulted—he had her rings!

He did not notice that the lights in the library went out immediately.

CHAPTER III

The following evening Jim Morlan ate his dinner in a restaurant frequented by those of the underworld. He was surly, mean. In the morning papers he had read of the robbery at the Blakeley house. Servants had been awakened, the story said, by the crashing of glass. It was evident that the thief had made his get away through a library window, and in a hurry. Evidently something had alarmed him.

That puzzled Jim Morlan to a great degree. Did not the woman—he supposed she was the daughter of the house—tell the police the truth?

And there was more to puzzle him. The robbery had been discovered by the servants just after the breaking of the window. And the safe was open, papers scattered about, currency, old jewelry, and rare coins missing.

Jim Morlan thought it all over again and cursed beneath his breath. There was some mystery, he supposed. At least he had the diamond rings, and they would repay him. He would wait for a few days, and then carry them to the fence. Perhaps that story in the newspapers was a trick of the police, a trap. They often had resorted to such tricks before.

Into the cafe came two men Jim Morlan knew well—"Burley" Bell, a pickpocket, and Harry Carls, a swindler. They sat down at the adjoining table and nodded at Morlan, and he nodded in return.

He gave them no attention for a time, and then suddenly he pricked up his ears.

"Have mercy, lady!" Bell was saying. "For Heaven's sake, lady, let me go!" Carls replied. "I'll go straight from now on!"

"Don't call the police, lady," said Bell. "I was driven to it! I swear I'll go straight!"

Jim Morlan's eyes bulged, and then his face turned red. He glanced at the others, and saw they were laughing.

"Great stuff!" Bell said to Carls. "It's the laugh of the district! This bird goes ahead and opens the safe and piles out the loot, and then Maizie comes along and gobbles it all in. And the boob gets away with a bunch of paste rings worth about fifteen dollars retail. My eye!"

"Let me go! I swear I'll run straight!"Carls grunted, tears of laughter running down his cheeks. "I was driven to it!"

"Here comes Maizie now," said Bell.

Jim Morlan glanced down the aisle from the corner of his eye. Along it, dressed in a neat blue suit, came the woman of the night before. She sat down at the table with Bell and Carls.

And then Bell got up and walked across to Jim Morlan.

"Come over and meet Maizie, Carls' girl," he said. "She's some moll, educated and all that. She'll tell you about a funny little trick she pulled last night, Morlan."

"Go to—" Morlan began.

"Oh, don't get rough about it!" Bell said. "You had it co-min' to you. No honor among thieves for you! You're a crooked crook, Morlan, but this'll finish you in this town. You're a huge joke to everybody in the know. Clever of you to open the safe and get out the loot for Maizie."

"I'll—"

"You'll take your medicine and clear out—or stay here and be laughed to death," Bell said, suddenly stern. "We've got enough to do watchin' cops, without watchin' a crooked crook, too. You were easy, Morlan. We had it all planned. We'd been watchin' you for a couple of weeks. Maizie played the game good, too. And that telelphone call to the cops—wires cut outside, Morlan, by yours truly. It may interest you to know that the swag brought Maizie a nice little roll. You may retain the paste rings, you boob!"

Bell turned and went back to the other table, said something under his breath, and Carls and the woman laughed.

"Have mercy!" said Carls. "I was driven to it! Let me go, lady, and I'll swear to run straight—"

Jim Morlan, in a rage, his dinner half eaten, grasped the check and his hat and hurried toward the cashier's cage. Behind him there was a gale of laughter. The eyes of the cashier were glistening.

"Some joke, Morlan," the cashier said. "Let me go, lady—"

Jim Morlan rushed out into the night. He knew when he was licked. He had a little money and there was a train leaving for the West in half an hour.

Jim Morlan caught the train.

PODDIN'S MISTAKE

CROUCHING in the darkness Poddin rubbed one hand over his bullet-shaped head, on which the hair was clipped close. Then he put on his dirty cap and pulled it down over his eyes, slouched forward, and continued down the street.

Poddin snarled as he walked, snarled like an angry wolf, and for no special reason except that he was betraying his true disposition. Years before, Poddin had caused himself to believe that it gave him courage to snarl at the world in general.

He was slipping along through the shadows cast by giant trees at the edge of the boulevard. The night before he had cached his revolver at a certain spot in front of a vacant lot, beneath a hedge that had not been trimmed for some time. He had been working at the other end of town the night before, but he reached the room he called home in a roundabout manner, and so had a chance to hide the gun. Poddin knew better than to carry a revolver except when it was absolutely necessary. A man of his ilk caught with a gun on his person was as good as on his way to prison.

It was almost midnight, and the section of the city which Poddin graced with his nocturnal presence was that of the better class of residences. Poddin was in new territory, and did not know whether he would have good fortune or not. He was killing time, after a fashion. He knew better than to be in another part of town where there had been several holdups recently, for the police were watching there. So he would strike here, if he got the opportunity. If he gained anything, it would put him so much ahead; he could not work at the other end of town for a time, anyway.

After a while, Poddin reached the spot where he had hidden his revolver. He made sure that there was nobody near, and then he took the gun from beneath the hedge and slipped it into his pocket. He knotted a black silk handkerchief around his neck in such a manner that it could be drawn up quickly over his face to the eyes, thus making an effectual mask. He was prepared.

There appeared to be a dearth of pedestrians. A few automobiles dashed by, but that was all. Poddin sat down in front of the hedge and began thinking that it was a fool stunt to be in this section of the city. Men did little walking at night up here. Those who were abroad were in their limousines.

To pass the time while he waited for a victim, Poddin began considering his past life, his present circumstances, and what the future held for him. He had been reared in the gutter, and at an early age had become the companion of crooks. He was without high standing, however, even in crookdom. For Poddin had been too shiftless to learn a crook's trade in the proper way. He hated mental exertion and a game of wits. Poddin's character was such that he deemed it the correct thing to step from a shadow, poke a gun under a man's nose, take his money and his watch, and make a get-away. That did not call for brain work. A sinister, treacherous thug was Poddin.

Twice he had done time, and at his previous appearance in court he had been warned that, if convicted again, he would be put away for life as a habitual criminal. Poddin's nature was such that he had no pals to aid him in case of disaster. He stood alone, and on insecure ground.

Take the present, for instance. The police were after him, and he knew it. They suspected him, rightly, of several highway robberies that had occurred within a month. He had seen a certain detective he knew loitering in his vicinity. The city was getting dangerous for him, and yet he did not want to go away and seek new fields.

Poddin thought that it would be an excellent thing if he was assured of bed and board and spending money for a time without doing anything nefarious to get them. If he only could avoid lawbreaking for a while, if he had money enough to be honest until the police forgot him to an extent and began watching others! But Poddin had not saved money. His holdups never netted him great sums. He had but a few dollars in his pocket, and that was all he had in the world.

If he could hold up a man in this section of town, he might get something besides small change, he thought. But it was midnight now, and there was nobody in sight. Poddin did not even see a policeman or a watchman. He thought for an instant of robbing a house; and then he dismissed that idea from his mind.

For Poddin knew nothing about burglary; he never had taken the trouble to learn the tricks of the trade, and so he feared it. It took nerve to enter another man's castle, facing probable death if discovery came, and Poddin did not possess nerve of that sort. Why, he did not even know how to enter a window without making a noise! And, once inside, he would not know how to protect himself or how to obtain articles of value.

No, he could not attempt to rob a house. It was highway robbery or nothing for Poddin. He was not clever enough to be a pickpocket, and he knew none of the tricks of other branches of crime. He was an ignorant holdup man, and that was all.

Poddin looked down the boulevard again, and then, far down the street, he saw a pedestrian approaching. For an instant a corner arc light flashed on a glistening shirt front. The man who approached Poddin was in evening dress.

"A swell," Poddin thought. Probably he would have a goodly sum on him, and an expensive watch, and a diamond ring of three or four carats. Poddin, you understand, was not well acquainted with the usages of polite society; he judged that any man who had the price would wear a diamond of three or four carats. He believed, with a certain man known to fame, that "them as has 'em, wears 'em."

Silently, Poddin gave thanks that the enemy was delivered into his hands. If he could manage to get a good roll, he could take it easy for a time and let the police watch in vain, he told himself. So Poddin drew back farther into the shadows, pulled up the handkerchief to screen the lower part of his face, and took the revolver from his pocket and held it ready.

CHAPTER II.

Wallace John Walkins, scion of the wealthy and socially prominent Walkins family, did not usually walk home at that hour of the night. But a man in love may do peculiar things, as Poddin learned that night.

Wallace John Walkins had been at the home of Gertrude Sanleigh for dinner. He had been paying particular attention to Gertrude for more than a year, and everybody in their social set said it was a match. Walkins, however, had not been sure, for Gertrude seemed to give him hope one moment and dash him upon the rocks of despair the next.

On this evening, however, Wallace John Walkins grew bold and asked the question, and Gertrude replied in the way he had hoped, and so they spent several hours out on the veranda, as lovers will, disregarding all other persons and the flight of time.

It was midnight when Walkins decided that it was certainly time for him to return to his father's house. Gertrude offered to send him in one of her father's cars, but Walkins decided that he would rather walk, since he would be walking on air, so to speak, and would not be fatigued. So he swung off down the boulevard, humming a song, dreaming of romance, and thinking not at all of the possibility of a holdup man stopping him and putting the muzzle of a gun beneath his nostrils.

Wallace John Walkins was twenty-eight. At the university he had been a leader in the more strenuous forms of athletics. He had been taught to act quickly in an emergency, to preserve his presence of mind, and he never had known the meaning of fear. It was reasonable to expect, then, that there would be a lively time when Poddin held him up.

Turning a corner Walkins made his way quickly along the tree-bordered boulevard toward his father's mansion. His hands were swinging at his sides. His overcoat was open. His hat sat on the back of his head, and that head was in the clouds.

Walkins came to the untrimmed hedge before an old estate, and went on inside the shadow it cast. Suddenly another shadow darted forward and stopped before him. There was a flash of the distant street light reflecting from the nickeled barrel of a weapon, and a gruff voice demanded:

"Hands up, bo! Elevate 'em, and don't try any funny business! Understand?"

At the command, Wallace John Walkins elevated his hands and stopped humming the song, for he was startled—not afraid, but startled. Poddin stepped forward, still covering his man, and ran a hand into the inside pocket of Walkins' coat. He clutched a wallet, transferred it to one of his own pockets, and fumbled to see whether Walkins carried a watch. The victim had not spoken a word, and Poddin supposed that he was badly frightened.

Then Wallace John Walkins went into action with a suddenness that disconcerted Poddin to an extreme. He swerved to one side, knocked the muzzle of the revolver away, caught Poddin behind the ear with his fist and almost knocked him flat, and then giving one more spring forward, hurled Poddin into the prickly hedge, yanked him forth again, slapped his face, and then held him with his arms pinioned at his sides.

'Trying to rob me, you rat?" asked Wallace John Walkins pleasantly. "Trying to hold me up on a night like this? It can't be done!"

Poddin gasped, but had nothing to say. He realized that he had made a mistake, that a white shirtfront did not mean lack of courage and strength. He began to whimper.

"I suppose you'll give me over to the police," he said. "Well, I can't help it."

"Why go around trying to rob people?" Walkins asked.

"It's the first time," Poddin lied. "I couldn't get work, and I was hungry. I sneaked the gun from a friend, and thought I'd turn bad. A man's got to eat."

Now Wallace John Walkins was a peculiar young man in some ways. It had been said of him that, during the usual trip around the world following his graduation from the university, he had consorted with all sorts of persons. He hauled Poddin forth into the light and looked him over.

"You have the appearance of a professional thug," Walkins said, "and I believe that you are, but I am willing to give you the benefit of the doubt."

"Then you'll let me go?" Poddin asked thankfully.

"You are not going to get off as easy as that," Walkins said. "Something of a scrapper, aren't you?"

"I guess I can take care of anybody in my own class."

"Ever been in a real home? Know how a gentleman lives, and all that?"

"I don't know much about such kinds of things, sir."

"Well, you're due to learn. I fired a valet yesterday because I caught him stealing. I'm going to take you home with me and give you the job. You certainly are not a professional valet, and so you should be refreshing."

"Thanks, sir; but I'm afraid that I couldn't fill the job," Poddin replied. "I wouldn't know what to do."

"I'll explain all that to you. And this isn't an offer of a job you can turn down," Wallace John Walkins informed him. "I am insisting that you take it. Understand? I'm going to give you a chance to go straight—and, believe me, you'll go straight, too! If I ever catch you stealing—you can guess what'll happen! Do you doubt that I can handle you?"

Walkins shook Poddin again.

"I guess you can handle me, sir," Poddin said.

"We don't want any guessing—understand? Are you sure that I can handle you?"

"I—yes, sir."

"Very good! I'm going to take you home right now, see that you take a bath and clean up, and then give you proper clothes. You'll probably frighten everybody else around the house into fits—for you do look like a thug—but they are used to these little fancies of mine. You will not be a prisoner—understand that! There'll be all sorts of things around that will be worth picking up—but the Lord help you if you pick up any of them without permission. I've got all kinds of money. If you stole from me and made a get-away, I'd drop everything else and take after you. I'd get you, and I'd do more than hand you over to the police—I'd handle you myself! That is understood? Come along, then!"

Grasping Poddin by the shoulder, Wallace John Walkins forced him along the street at a rapid rate. Poddin found his brain working at top speed for the first time in his life. This wouldn't be so bad, he decided.

As valet to Wallace John Walkins—Poddin did not know his name as yet, but he realized he was a gentleman of means—he would be able to keep away from the police for some time to come. He could play at being honest and grateful to Walkins for giving him a position, and then, at the proper time, he could take things of value from the Walkins house and seek other climes, there to live on the fat of the land for a time.

He continued to whimper, however, until Walkins commanded that he cease. They walked for several blocks, and finally turned in at a magnificent mansion and went to the front door. A butler opened it, though it was almost one o'clock in the morning.

"I have brought home a new valet," Walkins told the butler.

"Very good, sir," the butler replied. But he did not look as if he thought it was very good. His nose curled toward the ceiling when he caught sight of Poddin, and then and there warfare was declared between the two.

Walkins took Poddin to his own suite, forced him to bathe, gave him some clothes, showed him the little room where he was to sleep, and instructed him as to his first duties in the morning.

Poddin looked around the suite in amazement. He saw many things that he considered worth stealing.

"I'm to sleep in there, without anybody watchin' me?" Poddin asked then.

"You are," Walkins answered. "I explained the thing to you, didn't I? I've got to have a valet, and you're elected. It's difficult to get a good one in these days, and so I have decided to train you from the ground up. If you feel like stealing things and making a get-away through one of the windows, help yourself. But you know what'll happen if you do!"

Walkins glared at him, and Poddin retired to the other room. He had no idea of stealing things and making a get-away so soon. He wanted to impress upon Walkins that he was grateful for the chance to go straight. He'd wait for some time, until he had gained the confidence of his employer, until he had discovered the things most worth stealing, and then he would make plans and get away with a big haul.

Poddin was further instructed in his duties the following day, and soon became a fixture, despite the fact that the rest of the Walkins family regarded him as a dangerous crook, and the other servants would have little to do with him. He learned his work well, and attended to it. And gradually he learned things about the Walkins household.

The family was very rich, he found. Wallace John Walkins was engaged to Gertrude Sanleigh, who also came from a family exceptionally rich. Moreover, it was a love match. There was considerable entertaining being done already, and the marriage was to be consummated within four months.

The Walkins family had a fortune in jewels, and Poddin learned that the gems were kept in a special safe in the wall of the library. That safe was electrified heavily; the man who touched it died, and alarms were sounded in half a dozen places at the same time. Poddin knew that it would be no easy task to get into that safe, but he thought that it could be done, if he bided his time and watched.

Two months passed. Poddin knew a great deal about the house now. He knew that, any time the members of the family were out, he could go through certain rooms and pick up articles worth several thousand dollars. But Poddin wanted bigger game.

He pretended to be grateful to Wallace John Walkins, and he did his work as well as he could. Poddin was playing the game. In reality, he hated Walkins for forcing him to be an honest man. Walkins had missed a roll of bills once, and the way in which he had looked at Poddin was enough to make Poddin's flesh creep. Poddin was glad when Walkins found the roll of bills in the library, where they had dropped from his pocket.

The jewel safe fascinated Poddin, for that was his goal. Now and then he had a chance to get downtown to his old haunts, and he made arrangements with a "fence" to buy jewels of value when he should be able to deliver them. Poddin was doing a great deal of thinking these days. Two things he had to know—the combination of that safe, and the location of the switch that turned on and off the deadly electric current.

For Poddin was going to do it all by himself; he did not care to call in a professional cracksman. It was ridiculously easy, Poddin decided. When he learned the two things he had to know, he would have only to await his opportunity, turn off the current, open the safe, take the jewels and make his get-away. Then he would laugh long and loudly at his employer.

CHAPTER III.

Very much in love was Wallace John Walkins, so much so that he was not his normal self. His father and mother, his sister and his young brother worshiped his fiancée, too. It was a happy household as the time for the wedding approached.

Then Poddin began to fear that he would fail, that Walkins would get married and dismiss him, and that he would have to leave the Walkins house without securing the jewels, and with only his wages as reward for his service there.

He succeeded in developing a sort of cunning, and he put forward his best efforts to keep from using his usual snarl. He felt sure that Walkins trusted him now, though Walkins looked at him peculiarly now and then.

"Well, how goes it, Poddin?" Walkins asked upon a certain morning, looking at Poddin closely.

"Very well, sir."

"Glad that you're running straight?"

"Yes, sir. I have peace of mind, sir," Poddin said.

"Um! Don't revert to type, Poddin, if you want to keep that peace of mind. I'm not quite sure of you yet. I think you'd like to run away. I'm to be married soon, as you know, and shall be gone on my honeymoon for three months, and I'm not sure what I'll do with you. I'll decide it later."

Poddin snarled after Walkins had left the room. He knew what he intended doing. He hated Walkins. He'd show Walkins that he wasn't to have his comings and goings bossed by any man!

He redoubled his efforts to learn the combination of the safe. Now and then he got a chance to enter the library, but seldom when there was nobody else in the big room. But there came a day when Walkins' mother was entertaining for the bride-elect and all the servants were called upon to prepare the rooms on the lower floor for the event.

Poddin maneuvered so that he was assigned to the library. He betrayed a particular adaptability for banking flowers and ferns in that room, and Mrs. Walkins, who considered that

Poddin was grateful to her son and worshiped him and wanted to see him happy, left Poddin alone in the library to finish the work while she took the other servants to the other rooms.

Poddin seized his chance. He arranged mirrors so that there was a continued reflection from the safe in the wall to a corner of the veranda outside. It took him some time, but it was not a difficult task after all. And when he had finished, he aided in the work to be done in other rooms, and finally went up the stairs to his master's quarters.

Walkins left to conduct his fiancée to the house. Poddin slipped out of the house and made for the veranda, for he had listened at the door of Mrs. Walkins' room and knew that she had about finished dressing. She would then descend and get certain jewels from the safe, Poddin knew, for that was her habit.

Poddin reached the veranda and made his way along it slowly. In time he reached a spot near the railing. He could not see the safe in the wall directly, but he could look into the corner of a mirror that reflected another mirror that showed the safe.

With a stub of pencil and a card in his hands, Poddin waited. Through the mirror he saw Mrs. Walkins enter the room and speak to her husband, who got up and went immediately to the safe. Now Poddin bent forward and watched closely.

It was even better and easier than he had dreamed. He saw every move of Mr. Walkins' hand; he read the combination as easily as if he had been standing beside the master of the house. Five minutes later Poddin was back in his proper place, and in the pocket of his waistcoat was a card upon which had been written the combination of the safe in the library wall.

The first part of his work was done, and for that Poddin felt glad. But the electrification of the safe puzzled him a great deal. He knew how dangerous it would be to touch the strong box if the current was turned on. And he did not know the location of the switch. Poddin watched closely for another week, but could not discover it. There were more entertainments for Gertrude Sanleigh, and Poddin made the discovery that the valet of a young gentleman of means about to commit matrimony has work to do.

Then came a day when he was obliged to help the other servants. Poddin made himself generally useful, so much so that he was given more downstairs work. Mrs. Walkins was going out that afternoon to a tea, and Poddin supposed that she would wear a few of her jewels. So he watched carefully, managing to keep near the library.

He observed Mrs. Walkins talking to her husband, and then, hiding behind portieres, Poddin saw Mr. Walkins go along the hall to an innocent-looking panel, press against it, saw an aperture, and an electric switch within a secret wall box. Walkins threw the switch, and then went to the library and got the jewels for his wife. Then he returned and put the switch back again.

Poddin had all the knowledge he required now. He had but to perfect his arrangements with the "fence," await an opportunity, and commit the crime he contemplated. He would be in no hurry about it. Within a few days the house would be in a turmoil because of the approaching wedding; he would not be watched so closely by Wallace John Walkins—and that would be the time.

He had only to press back that panel, throw the switch and thus turn off the current, work the combination of the safe, take the jewels, close the safe and throw back the switch—and he would have a fortune in his hands.

He had another reason, too, for waiting. Wallace John Walkins had let it become known that his present to his bride would be a diamond necklace worth more than fifty thousand dollars. Poddin wanted to get that necklace, if possible. Then he could live as a man of means for the remainder of his life.

For he had his get-away planned perfectly. He would commit the robbery at night and at a time when it would be easy to get away from the house. He would go immediately to the "fence," who would be notified beforehand and would have money ready to purchase a part of the jewels. The money and the remainder of the jewels in his possession, Poddin would hurry to a suite of rooms he had rented, his landlady believing that he was a traveling man away from home a great part of the time. There he would change clothes and alter his appearance as much as possible. Having done that, Poddin would take a local train to a small station up the river. There he would engage an automobile and drive to a certain resort not far away. After that, he had two plans, depending upon what day the robbery was committed. One was to catch a steamship for a South American port, and the other was to go to Halifax and ship from there to a European city.

"She's sure some plan!" Poddin told himself. "That holdup of mine's goin' to turn out pretty good at that! Grateful to him, am I, because he helped me go straight? I'll show him!"

Poddin remembered that he had heard a man say once that ingratitude always is punished. The remembrance startled him for a moment, and then he laughed at his fears. He'd show Wallace John Walkins! If the bride was to have a diamond necklace, Wallace John Walkins would have to buy a second one. But he could afford it.

CHAPTER IV.

It was two days before the wedding when Poddin's chance came. Upon that evening there was a reception at the Walkins residence in honor of the bride-elect. And Poddin knew that the diamond necklace had arrived and had been placed in the safe in the library wall.

He helped Wallace John Walkins with his greatest skill that night.

"I think I'll leave you here, Poddin, while I'm on my honeymoon," Walkins told him. "My father will give you your wages. When I return, I'll need you again in your old capacity. While I'm gone, you just behave yourself and keep my rooms in order. Run away if you like—but remember what'll happen if you do!"

Poddin smiled sinisterly after Walkins had left the room. So Walkins thought he was afraid, did he? He'd have the laugh on Walkins before long. For this was the night Poddin intended to make his move. He had informed the "fence" and everything was in readiness.

He remained upstairs during the early evening, but he watched as the guests left, and he knew that Gertrude Sanleigh had remained to spend an extra hour with the family, and that Wallace John Walkins would take her home.

Poddin managed to get down the stairs and secrete himself in a position where he could watch the library.

"I'm going to give you a glimpse of it now," he heard Walkins saying to Gertrude Sanleigh.

The unwilling valet dodged back behind the portieres. He watched Walkins go into the hall, open the panel, and throw the electric switch. He saw him return to the library and open the safe, and take from it a jewel box.

Poddin almost gasped as the diamond necklace was held up to the light. The little bride-to-be clapped her hands like a child to express her delight. For a moment they looked at the necklace, and then Walkins returned it to the safe. Poddin hurried noiselessly up the stairs. An hour later he helped Walkins prepare for bed.

Until about two o'clock in the morning Poddin waited, and then he dressed quietly and went out to slip down the stairs. He had an electric torch in one pocket, a revolver in another pocket. He was snarling once more; he was his old self now. He did not fear the consequences of ingratitude. He wanted that fortune in gems. He'd teach Wallace John Walkins not to take a holdup man into his home and force him to do honest work!

It was all so simple that Poddin felt like leaving a note for Walkins, telling how easy it had been. But he knew better than to do that. He stopped at the bottom of the stairs to listen, hiding behind the portieres. There was no sound in the house.

Poddin had discovered much since taken into the house. He knew, for instance, how to disengage the electric burglar alarm that was attached to the doors and windows. He disconnected it now and raised a front window cautiously.

Then he hurried back to the hall and stood there for a minute or so, listening intently. He heard nothing to alarm him. He went down the hall noiselessly and stopped before the proper panel in the wall. He flashed his electric torch now, and pressed around the edge of the panel until he touched the spring. The panel slid back. Poddin flashed his torch again, quickly, for he did not like to make too much light. He saw the big electric switch before him, and quickly swung it up. Then he closed the panel again.

Poddin almost chuckled now. Force him to go straight, would they? Ingratitude be hanged! They could only blame themselves, he decided. Wallace John Walkins was to pay the price for trying to turn a criminal into an honest fellow.

Back through the hall Poddin went, making not the slightest noise. He stopped now and then to listen, and finally he came to the door of the library and opened it cautiously. He closed it behind him, stood against it to listen once more, and then went across the room cautiously to the panel behind which the safe rested.

Poddin had a touch of nervousness now, and he hesitated long enough to make an attempt to shake it off. He fumbled in his pocket and got the card upon which he had written the combination. But he would not need it unless nervousness caused him to forget, for he had memorized that combination long ago.

He flashed his torch and opened the wall panel before the safe. The door of the jewel safe was before him, and again Poddin almost chuckled because the theft was going to be so easy. He remembered how he had obtained the combination, how he had watched Wallace John Walkins betray the hiding place of the electric switch.

Once more he flashed the torch, and caused the light to play on the dial of the safe. He glanced at the card upon which he had written the combination, chuckled again, and then looked up at the dial. His hand went out carefully, and he grasped the knob.

And then it seemed to Poddin that a million lightning bolts struck him at the same time, that his life story flashed before him in an instant, that he took leave of a familiar country and came upon a new one in the twinkling of an eye!

A gong sounded, an alarm rang. Servants, suddenly awakened by the clamor, armed themselves according to orders and rushed toward the library.

Wallace John Walkins was one of the first persons to arrive on the scene. Stretched on the floor before the safe, lay Poddin, dead.

He had made his plans well, and he had made, also, one fatal mistake. He had neglected to take into consideration, the fact that a young man very much in love, and to be married within forty-eight hours, is likely to be rather forgetful.

Wallace John Walkins, having given his bride-to-be a glimpse of the magnificent necklace, had taken her home afterward—forgetting to turn on again the current that protected the safe.

And so Poddin, the ungrateful, when, he threw the switch and believed that he had made things safe, had, in reality, thrown the current on instead of off, and his life had paid the forfeit.

DIAMONDS, DIRT, AND DUTY

HE felt his heart pounding against his ribs, and "Stubby" Lade knew that his breath was coming in quick little gasps. He made an ineffectual attempt to overcome these indications of fear. He gulped and licked at his dry lips and closed his hands into fists, until the nails bit into the palms. Again he told himself that there could be no danger at all.

For a moment he had a sick feeling down in the pit of his stomach. His lips were trembling beyond his control, and his eyes seemed to burn. He drew in a deep breath, held it for a time, and then expelled it slowly. But the act seemed to have no beneficial effect; he only seemed to tremble the more.

"There ain't any sense in it!" Lade told himself in a hoarse whisper. "I ain't a softy, am I? And what's the difference between this and any other kind of a trick?"

But he knew that there was a great difference, for he could sense it. He felt like a man embarking on a new career, embarrassed by unusual surroundings, fearful of the outcome.

Stubby Lade was a man outside the pale of lawful society; at the same time he had not been admitted fully to the underworld. He was too bad to be called a decent, honest citizen, and not bad or clever enough to be known as an out-and-out crook. It was a situation, Stubby Lade had found, that had innumerable disadvantages. Being neither fish nor fowl is no joke!

For some years he had managed to acquire a precarious living by being a sneak thief of the most despised sort. He had robbed men stupefied with drink, and he had stolen from residences where the back doors accidentally had been left unlocked. He had snatched a woman's purse when the opportunity offered, and had been attempting to follow the game of living by his wits when those who knew him best declared he had no wit at all.

But they made a grave error in that. Stubby Lade had cunning and brains. But it had seemed impossible for him to apply his brains and cunning correctly to the problems of existence.

He needed a firm guiding hand, and there was no crook of recognized standing who cared to couple up with him.

A few days before, a certain Head-liner in the vaudeville of crime had sneered in the face of Stubby Lade and suggested that he go forth and acquire a reputation. He had made the remark that anybody could rob a baby or an intoxicated man or snatch a woman's purse. He succeeded, without realizing it, in making Stubby Lade thoroughly ashamed of himself.

Following some days of serious thought, Stubby Lade had decided to make something of himself in the world of crookdom, or meet with disaster in the attempt, disaster meaning capture, incarceration, trial, and sentence.

He had considered a career as a burglar at first, but had turned aside from that with the conviction that successful burglary called for certain experience and knowledge, both of which he lacked.

His clothes would not qualify him to turn swindler and go after the rich game. So he decided, finally, that he would start as a holdup man and gather enough money in that way to outfit himself properly to turn to the finer art of swindling.

Stubby Lade was ambitious for the first time in his life, but his ambitions ran in illegal and nefarious channels. He wanted to make a name for himself and become a terror to the police. Success and prosperity were his goal.

What was there to prevent him from becoming as notorious as Stalley, for instance? Stalley was feared and respected by the local underworld. He always worked alone, and he always succeeded. When a big trick was turned and nobody knew who had turned it, everybody suspected Stalley and grinned when they saw him. The police had been after Stalley for years, and that was all the good it had done them.

Stalley was pointed out as he walked along the streets, and it was Stalley who attracted the particular attention of Detective Michael Murphy, the bloodhound of the department. There was a continual game of hide and seek between Stalley and Murphy. Stubby Lade told himself that some day in the future he would be a Stalley and would have a man like Michael Murphy after him, and then he would make Murphy look foolish.

A holdup man does not rank high in the world of crime. The burglar takes his life in his hands when he invades the property of another, but the holdup man takes only a mean advantage. He steps from his place of concealment and presents the business end of a weapon at his victim, catching him off guard and giving him not the slightest fighting chance. In a way the professional holdup man is an errant coward.

Stubby Lade felt that it was otherwise this evening, however. It seemed to Lade that to be a holdup man called forth all the courage a human being could possess. He cursed himself for a craven and tried to tell himself that his nervousness was because this was his first attempt, but he could not bring himself to the deed.

All his preparations had been carefully planned. There had not been a holdup in the district for some time, and the police were not very active. And this was the evening when the big factory, down on the waterfront, paid off its men, and many of them lived in the neighborhood.

At the mouth of a dark alley Stubby Lade had taken up his position. It was a bit after nine o'clock, and many of the men from the factory were going to the stores to pay bills and purchase provisions, and others were hurrying to the pool halls and other resorts of the district.

Crouching a short distance from the mouth of the alley, Lade could look down the slanting street and see who approached. All that he had to do was pick a victim, work swiftly, and then dart back into the dark alley. There were fifty ways of escape within as many yards.

Three times Stubby Lade had picked a victim. Slipping up over his chin and almost to his eyes the dark handkerchief which he had looped around his neck, he had crept along the wall to the walk. And three times, his heart pounding at his ribs, he had crept back again, to let his prospective victim proceed down the street, unmolested and unsuspecting.

Now he crouched in the darkness and cursed himself for a coward and a fool. There was no reason in it, he declared to himself. He had planned everything perfectly. He wore a soft, black cap, and, as he would dart down the alley after the crime, he could throw it into an ash can and substitute a hat, which he had placed in a certain position against the wall. That would help wreck any description his victim might give.

He would drop his revolver into a hole at the end of a shed. It was a gun which he had stolen many months before and it could not be traced to his ownership. He wore gloves to keep from leaving his ringer prints on the gun, and he would drop the gloves into the hole with the weapon.

He had planned at least a dozen methods of exit from the alley, and would use the one that happened to be the most convenient under the circumstances. One led to the street in front, another to the rear door of a pool hall, and a third into a lodging house. Lade had been as careful with the arrangements for his first holdup as a greater crook would have been in planning a raid on the sub-treasury.

Mentally Lade lashed himself. If he failed tonight he always would be a common good-for-nothing. It was his big chance to convince himself that he had real stuff in him! Better to try and fail, no matter what happened, than never to make the try at all!

A little later, he knew, the street would be more crowded, and more persons would be passing the mouth of the alley. And the factory workmen had their money when they went down the street, but they would not have very much of it left when they returned. Now was the proper time to do the work. Half an hour later, fifteen minutes later possibly, would be too late.

Nerving himself as much as possible he once more crept along the wall in the darkness, going toward the alley's end. He came to a spot from where he could look down the slanting street. Half a block away a man was crossing diagonally beneath an arc light. Lade could see him plainly.

He had observed this man often before, though he never had exchanged words with him. But he knew him and his reputation. He was short, heavy-shouldered, a bachelor who spent his money as fast as he earned it.

Now, Lade guessed, he was hurrying toward the busier, brighter street above, his wages for the week burning a hole in his pocket. He would spend the money in the pool halls, else waste it playing cards in some back room. He was the logical victim for Stubby Lade, a proper man for Lade to use in starting his career as a real crook.

Somehow Lade had a feeling that it was his last chance. Here was where he either proved himself, or convinced himself that he always would be nothing, even in the world of sordid crime. It was a crisis, a moment wherein Lade was compelled to meet the situation, face to face. A decision could not be avoided.

He pulled the handkerchief well up over his chin again, almost to the eyes, tugged at his cap and took the revolver from his pocket. Crouching in the dense darkness against the wall, his heart still pounding at his ribs, he waited.

His prospective victim came rapidly nearer, walking swiftly. Looking through a hole in the wall, Lade could see up the street in the opposite direction. There was nobody approaching. He had things his own way!

CHAPTER II
THE BREATH OF DISASTER

WITH a brave attempt to concentrate on the work before him, Lade told himself that it would be over almost immediately. He had thought about it so much and had planned so extensively and had lived through the scene so many times that he would act mechanically.

The prospective victim was walking close to the row of dark buildings, and this made it easier for Lade. The latter crept closer to the end of the alley and glanced up the street again to make sure that nobody had turned the corner and would be able to see what occurred.

Certainly Lade felt shaky, but not so nervous as he had been. He had braced himself for the ordeal at last, and he told himself that, this first holdup accomplished successfully, the ones to follow would be as nothing.

His intended victim was very close to him now. "Lade stood up against the wall and bent forward. He watched the approaching man cautiously. He still walked swiftly, and it was evident to Lade that his thoughts were on the brightly lighted street ahead.

Then the moment came, almost before Lade realized it. He took a quick step forward, the hand grasping the revolver came up, and he spoke in a hoarse voice that was far from being his own. "Put 'em up!" he commanded.

The victim stopped abruptly, and a look of astonishment, that Lade could not see in the darkness, swept across his face. He gulped, and, as Lade jammed the muzzle of the weapon against his stomach, he began putting up his hands.

Then the unexpected happened, and Stubby Lade discovered that it is rather disconcerting, to say the least, to rehearse a scene repeatedly and then have the scene go wrong.

The victim suddenly lurched to one side, shrieked, seized the revolver and wrenched it from Lade's grasp with one hand, and with the other grasped the handkerchief and jerked it downward. It happened before Lade was aware that the man was resisting.

"I know you," said the man.

In that instant real fear seized Lade. He went to pieces thoroughly. He jerked backward and found himself free. He turned and plunged into the dark alley, and the intended victim plunged after him.

Fortunately there was nobody else near. But the other man kept close to his heels. Lade did not have the courage to turn and fight, and he remembered that his revolver had been wrenched from his hand, and it was possible that the other still possessed it. The next instant Lade knew that it was so. There was a crack behind him, and a bullet whistled past his head. He darted quickly to one side as the second crack of the weapon came. Then the other man charged down upon him.

Lade had sense enough left to throw out a foot, and the other tripped and crashed headlong. The next instant Stubby Lade was through a little gate in the wall and running noiselessly between two buildings. He tossed his cap and gloves aside, snatched up his soft hat from where he had left it, thrust it on his head and then ran on.

He was trying to reach the street, or the rear door of the lodging house. If he could get into the latter he could walk calmly through the front hall, and everybody would think that he had been in the building, visiting an acquaintance. He happened to know several men who lived in the house.

But suddenly he found the narrow way blocked. Somebody opened the gate that fed to the street and stepped inside. Lade stopped in his tracks. Behind him he heard the man whom he had attempted to rob, bellowing, and he knew that his manner of escape from the alley had been discovered. There were other voices in the alley now, too, other pursuers.

The breath of disaster was blowing in his face. He was like a rat in a trap. He remembered the man's cry: "I know you!" He sensed that he was lost, that the big gray prison up the river soon would have him for an inmate, and that the real crooks in the district would curl their lips when his name was spoken and mention something about amateurs and bunglers.

Against the wall of the building he waited, uncertain what course to pursue. There was a door behind him, and he knew that it led into the lower rear hall of the cheap lodging house. He decided that it would be best to open that door and enter and hurry through to the street. But his victim had recognized him! There was some uncertainty, of course, but, if he really had recognized him, Lade had no alibi.

He could not hesitate. So he turned toward the door, and it was opened in his face. Lade recoiled. The man who had opened it was the great Stalley.

"Come in, quick!" Stalley exclaimed.

Without making a reply, Lade sprang inside, and Stalley slammed the door shut behind him. "This way!" Stalley commanded.

Lade did not know what to make of it, but he gulped again, this time from relief, instead of fear, and tried to brace his shoulders, and he followed the great Stalley along the hall and toward the front of the building and the street.

It seemed to Stubby Lade that his brain was refusing to work. He did not know why Stalley had spoken to him, and could not understand why he was following Stalley without a word, like a dog following his master.

Stalley was intending to lead him to the street, Lade saw. He had a sudden terror of the street. Disaster might wait for him there. He was afraid of bright lights, of people. He stopped still, and Stalley turned and saw the look in his face. "Buck up!" Stalley commanded. "Leave it to me!"

His words heartened Lade, though Lade scarcely knew the reason why they should. Yet he seemed to have faith in Stalley. He followed Stalley to the front door, and they stepped out into the busy street, to stand just to one side of the door, as though in deep conversation.

"Get that scared look out of your face!" Stalley commanded in a whisper. "Let 'em howl, and leave it to me! You're a man, ain't you? Show me, then!"

Lade's nerves seemed to undergo a reaction at that instant. Suddenly he felt cool and collected. He heard a noise in the passageway between the two buildings, and then he saw the man whom he had attempted to rob coming quickly along the walk with Detective Michael Murphy.

For the first time in his life, Lade was not afraid of Detective Murphy. He always had been afraid of him and his reputation, even when he had no cause to be. And, now that he had cause, it seemed peculiar that he did not cut and run.

He leaned against the corner of the building, puffing at the cigarette which Stalley had given him and listening to the great Stalley talk. He knew that Detective Murphy and the other man had come to a stop a few feet away, but he did not turn from Stalley.

"Lade, where have you been for the last half an hour?" Murphy asked suddenly.

Lade whirled around quickly, a look of surprise in his face. But, before he could answer, Stalley spoke.

"He's been with me, Murphy, trying to make a touch, if you want to know," Stalley said. "Gunning for small game now, are you?"

Detective Murphy's eyes grew narrow, and he chewed at the corner of his lip, a bad sign. "This gent says that Lade tried to hold him up at the end of the alley a few minutes ago," Murphy said.

"The gent must be mistaken," declared Stalley, "unless it was more than half an hour ago. You know me, Murphy. I don't nurse small-time crooks."

"Yes, I know you, Stalley. And I'm surprised to see you hooked up with a man like Lade." There was sarcasm in the detective's voice, and Stalley's face flushed.

"What do you mean, hooked up with him?" Stalley demanded with a sneer. "He came to me to make a touch, I said, or to try to make one. I don't hook up with anybody, Murphy, and you ought to know it! I don't need any pals."

The man whom Lade had tried to rob spoke. "I felt sure that it was this man," he said. "I've seen him hanging around a lot and know his face. And the man who tried to hold me up looked like him, but he wore a cap."

"So you're not certain, after all?" Detective Murphy asked. "You want to be careful how you go around accusing people. If this fellow amounted to anything he could make it pretty hot for you."

"Murphy, I gave you credit for having more sense," Stalley declared. "You've seen Lade around a lot, and you know how to read men. Do you think he's got nerve enough to hold up anybody?"

Lade pretended to start a protest, but Stalley laughed. "Lade is about the last person in the town who would try to stick up a man," the great Stalley continued. "When it comes to having nerve, Lade isn't a howling example of perfection. If you were to suspect me, now—"

"Aw, shut up!" Detective Michael Murphy replied. "And you go along about your business!" he said to the man who had made the complaint. "You didn't lose anything, and you got the crook's gun, so you've nothing to worry about. We'll look around, of course, and keep our eyes open."

Lade's intended victim hurried on down the street toward his belated card game, convinced that he was fortunate not to be arrested for something himself. Stalley lighted a fresh cigarette. He met the eyes of Detective Michael Murphy squarely and without fear in his own, and then he turned toward Lade and went on talking.

"I haven't any money to throw away, Lade, as I was saying before we were interrupted. If you can show me that you really have landed a job, I'll stand good for your room rent and lend you five to buy eats. That's the best that I can do. I don't see why you should come to me, anyway. We haven't been such great pals."

Detective Murphy snorted his disgust and went on up the street to attend to his business. Stalley continued his aimless talk, and Lade listened, wondering what was coming, trying to understand what had happened.

"I guess it is safe now," Stalley said after five minutes. "You come back into the house and up to my room. I want to have a little talk with you, Lade."

Following the big man through the door and up the stairs, Lade suddenly felt elated. The great Stalley had saved him, for some reason unknown to Lade, and not only that, but also the great Stalley had asked him to come up to his room and had said that he wanted to talk!

There were dozens of crooks in the district who would have felt highly honored to get such an invitation from Stalley, and it had come to him, a nobody in the world of crime! The breath of disaster had been but a breath and not a gale!

CHAPTER III
A NEW COMBINATION.

STALLEY snapped on the lights, waved Lade to a chair and closed and locked the door. Then he sat down near Lade and for a moment looked at him without speaking.

In his nervousness Lade began to inspect the room casually. He was somewhat surprised. The great Stalley, it appeared, was not an ordinary crook. He had books and pictures, and, though Lade did not know much about such things, he sensed that the books and pictures were good.

"Lade, I've been watching you for some time," Stalley said presently.

"Watchin' me?" Lade asked.

"Yes. It amuses me to watch a man now and then and, perhaps, try to figure out what makes him run. You're a queer misfit, Lade, really."

The other man did not resent the statement, because he felt that Stalley had spoken the truth.

"I watched you tonight," Stalley declared. "I saw you in that alley, saw that you could not quite make up your mind to tackle the job. That is why you didn't succeed, Lade."

"I—I don't know what was the matter," Lade declared.

"You've got nerve, Lade, and more intelligence than the folks around here think. I've seen you do some clever things, and I know that you can think quickly in a crisis. Yet you don't amount to anything."

"I never seem to be able to get a start," Lade replied.

"I know. There are a lot of men like that. You've got the goods and don't know how to deliver them. I've an idea you're a pretty decent sort, Lade. What do you know about me?"

"Not much," Lade admitted. "I know what everybody else knows and thinks, that you always work alone, and that you're too clever for the cops."

"Sometimes people think they know things when they do not," said the great Stalley. "For a starter, I don't work alone."

"You don't?" Lade asked.

"I never advertised my partner, and I never worked with but one man. He died two months ago from an attack of pneumonia. I've been looking for his successor."

A sudden wild hope was born in the breast of Stubby Lade, but, in the same instant, he told himself that he was a fool to hope.

The great Stalley continued. "You'd make a good gun if you had somebody to give you a tip, now and then," he said. "I wonder, if you had a pal. if you could be loyal."

"Try me!" Lade said hoarsely. "You saved me tonight."

"That wasn't anything. You acted like such a boob that I wanted to see you have another chance. If that holdup had been planned in conjunction with somebody else, you'd probably have pulled it off all right. How would you like to work with me?"

"Great!" Lade declared.

"Anybody got any strings on you?"

"Nobody."

"Acquainted with Burlen?"

"I know him when I see him," Lade replied.

"And you know all about him, I suppose. Burlen is the boss of the underworld in these parts, if you listen to people talk. But he never bossed me. Burlen sits back and looks wise and takes a big percentage and now and then puts up fifty bucks for bail, if one of the boys gets arrested for fighting, or some little thing like that. But Burlen never made a deal with me."

"I've heard that."

"I don't need Burlen's help, and I refuse to be known as one of Burlen's slaves," Stalley said. "He tried to get me once or twice, and then he gave it up as a bad job. I could be his right-hand man if I wished, in the place of Dan Clanner. Know Clanner?"

"When I see him," said Lade. "I know that he's Burlen's right-hand man, of course."

"And he'll be the goat if Burlen ever finds himself in trouble," Stalley declared. "So I have nothing to do with Burlen, and anybody who works with toe must take the same stand."

"I understand," Lade said.

"I'm a peculiar sort of crook," Stalley said frankly. "I don't have to be a crook. There's an estate that sends me mine every quarter. But I've few friends and no relatives that I can recognize as such, and so I play the wild game for the excitement and adventure and sport in it."

"Yes, sir," said Lade.

"I need a helper. I've taken a fancy to you, simply because you know that you don't amount to anything and you're ambitious. You're not like these loud-mouthed bullies who run around telling everybody how tough and clever they are. And you've had sense enough not to hook up with some gangster and run errands for him."

"If you'd take me on—" Lade began.

"Understand one thing!" Stalley got up and bent over the table, and his eyes blazed. "If you ever play me false I'll—"

"I wouldn't!" Lade exclaimed.

"And there's another thing. I'm boss, always!"

"Of course!"

"All right! I'll get you a room here, and you move tomorrow. Got any money?"

"A couple of dollars." Stalley tossed him a couple of bills. "Get some new clothes the first thing in the morning," he commanded. "Then move here in the afternoon. You'll have the room next to mine. Somebody's in it now, but he won't be at noon tomorrow."

"How about Murphy?" Lade asked.

Stalley grinned. "I'm glad to see that you've got some sense," he said. "I knew you had, and I hope you get those wits of yours working and keep them at it. Of course, Murphy, or any other cop, might get suspicious if suddenly you blossomed out in good clothes and always had money, with no visible means of support."

"That's what I meant," said Lade.

"I'll fix that. Know the big warehouse, three blocks down the street?"

"Yes."

"The superintendent is a friend of mine," Stalley said. "In the morning he'll put you on the pay roll as a night watchman. He'll be ready at all times to say that you're on the job. The pay is good, too. Only you'll not draw the pay. You'll be free to do as you please nights and sleep days. If anybody should go nosing around, it'll either be your night off, or else you're sick. Understand?"

"Sure!" said Lade.

"Better take a big think before you shake hands on it," said Stalley. "I expect my man to stick to me through all kinds of weather."

"You needn't be afraid that I'll not."

"If you shouldn't—" The great Stalley did not complete the sentence, nor did he have to do so. Stubby Lade understood what he meant.

"I'll stick!" Lade said. "You can be sure of that! I don't amount to anything alone. You saved me tonight I'll do just as you say and work hard. And I'll be careful!"

"Especially the last," Stalley said smilingly. "You'd better be careful, always. Because, Lade, I'm not going to keep you in the dark as I did my other pal. It won't be long until everybody around here will know that you're working with me. Detective Mike Murphy will be out trying to get us. He'll try through you."

"I'm not afraid of Murphy!" Lade declared. "But he's a wise cop, and so I'll be careful."

"Good enough!" the great Stalley said. "That's all for tonight, Lade. Do as I told you, and well have a little talk tomorrow afternoon. Your room here will be ready for you when you come."

Two minutes later an elated Stubby Lade was hurrying through the hall toward the stairs that led to the street. Stalley remained sitting in the room, smiling to himself. He knew that Lade would be loyal, he told himself, because gratitude is the basis of a lot of stuff that people call loyalty.

CHAPTER IV
OFFERS REFUSED

FOUR months of association with the great Stalley made a new man of Stubby Lade.

From the first the new combination was highly successful. Given confidence in himself Lade had brilliant ideas that delighted Stalley. They became more than partners, they became friends.

It became noised through the underworld that the despised Lade had become a brilliant genius and was the great Stalley's right-hand man. The attitude toward Lade changed, but he did not seem to sense it. He did not crave popularity, it appeared. He thought of nobody but Stalley, lived but to serve Stalley.

Detective Michael Murphy was well aware of the state of affairs. He said nothing, but his eyes narrowed whenever he saw Stalley or Lade. Detective Murphy was waiting for the proper opportunity. He would get Stalley sooner or later, he told himself. Lade was small fry compared to Stalley.

The partners turned several tricks that were the talk of the town. That is, it was supposed that they turned them. There was no evidence to connect them with the crimes, but their cleverness, the way in which they were accomplished and the fact that no other crook boasted of them, were enough to convince the knowing that Lade and Stalley had scored.

While Detective Murphy and his comrades watched and waited, there were others interested in Stalley and Lade, too. Burlen was one of them. On a certain morning, some four months after Stalley and Lade had formed their partnership, Burlen called to him Dan Clanner, his right-hand man.

Burlen ran a wholesale and retail tobacco establishment and made it pay a handsome profit. But it was only a blind for his more nefarious work, and everybody knew it. Yet the police never had been able to get anything on Burlen.

Dan Clanner found Burlen behind his big desk, chewing at an unlighted cigar, a frown on his face. Clanner noticed the frown, but he did not betray his own agitation.

"Sit clown!" Burlen growled.

Dan Clanner sat down and helped himself to a cigar from the open box on the desk. He lighted it and puffed and waited for his master to speak. Burlen suddenly tossed his half-chewed cigar away and sat up straight in his chair.

"What do you happen to know about Stalley and Lade?" he demanded of Dan Clanner,

"Don't know anything for sure, except that they are working together."

"Everybody knows that," Burlen replied.

"I haven't been trying to get any dope on them, boss. I understood they didn't belong."

"They don't!" Burlen snarled. "That's what is bothering me. Stalley and Lade are pulling off some of the biggest things of the last ten years. They're so infernally clever that the cops can't even get a line on their work. Stalley is the best man I've ever seen."

"He's clever, all right."

"And he and his partner are the only good men who are not hooked up with us," Burlen declared.

"Do you want 'em?" Clanner asked.

"Of course I want them! Getting them is a different proposition. Stalley likes to be an outsider. But I'll make a try."

"Any orders, boss?"

"Yes. I want to see Stalley. See that he comes here. If I can't deal with Stalley, perhaps I can deal with Lade. Get Stalley here and then stick around."

Dan Clanner hurried from the office and wandered around the district. It was the middle of the afternoon when he happened to run across Stalley. He waited his chance and finally got to speak to Stalley when no other man was near.

"Burlen wants to see you," he said.

"Does he?" Stalley asked. "That's interesting. And what does Burlen want to see me about?"

"I guess you'll have to ask him that," Dan Clanner said. "I'm just his messenger boy. He'll be at his office all afternoon, he's there now."

"I'm too busy doing nothing to run in and see him," said Stalley grinningly.

"I'd do it if I was you," said Dan Clanner. "Of course if you're afraid to talk to him—"

"Afraid of a thing like Burlen?" Stalley asked. "I'll go and see him this minute, and a lot of good it will do him!"

Stalley was smiling when he was ushered into Burlen's office. He took the chair Burlen offered, accepted a cigar, and refused a drink of contraband liquor.

"I understood from Dan Clanner that you wanted to see me about something in particular," Stalley said. "Not having anything more important to do I dropped in. What's the answer?"

Burlen's eyes narrowed, but he managed to keep a pleasant look in his face. He knocked the ashes from his cigar and bent forward. "Stalley," he said, speaking in low tones, "I have to hand it to you and that partner of yours. You're clever!"

"Thanks," Stalley said.

"I know blamed well that a few things that have happened in the last three or four months could be explained by you if you cared to explain them. I reckon that we understand each other."

"Possibly," Stalley said. "I understand you better than you understand me."

"We never seemed to get along," Burlen said. "I don't know why we shouldn't. Working together we might be able to pull off some good things."

"Yes?"

"In a way we're working against each other now. You could help me a lot, and I could help you. I know a dozen little affairs, right this minute, that can't be pulled off because I haven't any friends who are clever enough. There's money going to waste, Stalley."

"A lot of it," Stalley agreed.

"Dan Clanner, just between ourselves, is the cleverest man I have, and he isn't clever enough. You can have his place, Stalley." Burlen leaned back in his chair and puffed at a fresh cigar. Stalley smiled again.

"Just what is your proposition?" Stalley asked.

"Come in with me," said Burlen. "You can be my right-hand man. We'll work together. I know things you do not know, and you know methods of which I am ignorant. I can show you a dozen ways to make big profits on the money you have to invest. And we'll keep pulling off new stunts, too. The cops can't touch you, and they can't touch me. If we were together we'd make them look like monkeys."

"How about Lade?"

"He's your pal, and he can continue to be," Burlen said.

Stalley removed his cigar from his lips and grinned. "Burlen, we can't make the deal," he said. "You may need me in your business, but I don't need you in mine. Lade and I keep our profits, we don't split them with any one else."

"No?" Burlen asked sneeringly.

"No! I guess that's all, Burlen!"

"Possibly not! I can take care of my friends, Stalley, and also my enemies."

"Threatening me, are you?" Stalley asked, laughing loud-ly. "You poor fool! If you, or any of your half-witted dupes, make a move against me you'll gee a pretty fight. Understand that! I can guess every trick of yours an hour before you think of it. I can foresee the workings of that poor, shriveled thing you call your brain. Burlen, you're not half so dangerous as you think!"

Stalley got up and moved toward the door. There he turned and grinned again. "Thanks for a good cigar," he said, "and a good laugh. You're some comedian, Burlen!"

Then he went out and closed the door softly after him, but Burlen could hear him chuckling. Burlen sat before the desk, his face almost purple with rage. He breathed heavily for a moment, and then he touched a button that would ring a bell and call Dan Clanner from the pool room in the rear.

Clanner entered and stood waiting.

"I want you to get that man Lade here," Burlen directed. "Get him as soon as you can, before Stalley has a chance to talk to him, and don't let Stalley know that you're bringing him here."

Dan Clanner knew that; he must succeed, for Burlen was in a dangerous mood. It took him less than an hour to find Lade. "Burlen wants to see you about something," Clanner said. "He is at his office now."

Four months before Lade would have thrilled at that information, but now it did not seem to touch him. Yet, the invitation was a mark of distinction, in a way. Lade, who thought he might learn something that would be of value to Stalley, went to Burlen's place with Clanner and was admitted to the sacred private office. It was the first time Lade had spoken to Burlen, the first time he had seen him near at hand. Yet Lade, who would have been timid four months before, being a new man now, accepted a cigar and waited calmly for what Burlen had to say.

"Lade, we all made a little mistake about you," Burlen began, "It was the general idea that you didn't amount to much, but I'll say now that you do."

"Thanks," Lade replied.

"I'd like to be your friend, Lade," Burlen went on. "I assume that you know a few things about me, and so you know that it means something to be my friend. I understand that you are hooked up with Stalley, As a matter of fact, you are the brains of the combination."

Burlen stopped to light his cigar afresh and let that bit of flattery sink in. It did not sink in, but Burlen did not know that. He bent forward again. "I assume that your association with Stalley is profitable," he said.

"Possibly."

"It should be. You furnish the brains. But Stalley is only one man, Lade. Suppose you were furnishing those brains of yours to me? You couldn't plan a thing, Lade, but what I'd have the men and women to carry it out. Not one man, but an entire gang. Any sort you demanded, Lade, burglars, con men, dips. You'd have a chance to use that brain of yours on big things, and the profits would be a lot bigger."

"Yeh?" Lade asked.

"I hate to see you throw yourself away on Stalley, Lade. Suppose a little slip came. Could Stalley protect you? Well, in such case I could. I've got lawyers lined up, I can furnish bail, I can manufacture evidence to suit the case. Think it over!"

"What's the idea?" Lade wanted to know.

"Come in with me, Lade. We can do some great things together. It'll be easy for you. Come in with me. Drop Stalley!"

Lade tossed his cigar away and got to his feet. His eyes were glowing. "Drop Stalley, eh?" he said. "Burlen, you poor fish! Stalley took hold of me when I was nothing better than a bum, and in four months he had shown me what I can make of myself. Drop Stalley? I'd drop you with a bullet first, Burlen! Think I haven't any sense? I'll bet you tried to get Stalley and couldn't. And now you think that you'll get me and so break up the combination. And you'd dump me, or have me railroaded, as soon as it was fixed. Burlen, you're a bum!"

"Talking big, are you?" Burlen inquired. "Feeling your oats because you've pulled off a few little tricks and got away with them? Either you're with me or against me, Lade! When a man is against me, I know how to handle him!"

Lade laughed. "Go ahead and try to handle me," he said. "I'm not afraid of you, Burlen." He went out and slammed the door. Burlen remained sitting before the desk, a picture of rage.

CHAPTER V
PLANS THAT FAILED

BURLEN had an only daughter, Elsie, a handsome woman of twenty-five. She had been reared in an unhealthy environment, and there were few things on the sordid side of life with which she was not acquainted; yet it was well known throughout the district that Elsie Burlen had a code of morals.

The father had kept the daughter more or less in the background. He felt that she was a sort of princess of crime and should not be allowed association with the common run of crooks. For the past year she had been traveling with an aunt, visiting the resorts of the country. Burlen wired for her to return immediately, and, during the week it took her to travel across the continent, he schemed and planned. Lade had never seen Elsie Burlen, he knew, Stalley had seen her, but only from a distance. Elsie was a beautiful woman and a clever one. If anybody could break the Stalley-Lade combination, and so weaken Stalley, she was the one.

It had been Elsie who had brought Dan Clanner to Burlen's side. Clanner was infatuated with the girl, but she despised him. Yet he remained loyal to Burlen because of her and continued to hope.

Now Elsie, Burlen believed, could bring Stalley to him in the same manner, or could play Stalley against Lade and break up their partnership.

It did not take Burlen long to state the business when his daughter was home and had rested from her journey. "You've been running around for a year or so, spending a lot of money," he told her. "Now I want you to do something for me in return."

He outlined the state of affairs as rapidly as possible, and then watched her as she thought it out.

"Do you really want Stalley in the gang?" she asked.

"Either in the gang or out of the way."

"And what do you want me to do?"

"You're a clever woman," Burlen said. "Two friends often fall out over a clever woman. If you could manage to get both of them interested in you, they'd quarrel in time. It's an old game."

"Perhaps this Stalley is too clever to fall for it," Elsie Burlen said.

"The cleverest men are the ones who fall for a woman's game," Burlen reminded her. "Of course, if you do not want to tackle the jab, if you think you could not get them interested—"

Elsie Burlen's face flushed. "You think that I could not?" she asked. It was a challenge she could not refuse. She did not rush matters. She went to work systematically and carefully. She contrived to meet both Stalley and Lade, but she did it in a manner perfectly natural, and she did not seem to pay particular attention to them when they did meet.

But both Lade and Stalley found that their paths crossed that of Elsie Burlen, now and then. They seldom met her when they were together. Stalley might meet her on the street and walk a block or so, Lade might see her in some store.

Within the month, however, both Stalley and Lade were interested in her, and each thought that the other man was not. They were commencing to grow infatuated. Elsie Burlen was using the old game of playing one against the other.

And then, when she deemed they were sufficiently infatuated, she thought that the time had come to let each man know that his partner was interested, too. That would bring about jealousy and distrust, she believed, and no partnership can survive distrust and jealousy. Stalley and Lade would separate, possibly hating each other. Stalley would join hands with Burlen, or Lade would, and so leave Stalley alone.

There came an afternoon when Stalley, meeting Elsie Burlen on the street, asked to escort her to a dance in the neighborhood the following evening.

"Can't," she said, smiling at him. "I promised to go with Mr. Lade."

"With Lade!"Stalley exclaimed. "I didn't know that you were well acquainted with Lade."

"You didn't know it?" she asked. "And he is your partner? Why, I know him as well as I do you, Stalley. We've been together a lot. It's funny he never mentioned it to you, and it isn't very complimentary to me."

Stalley continued up the street, thinking deeply. He went to his room, lighted his favorite pipe, and thought some more. It looked as though Lade had been deceiving him. Lade scarcely had mentioned Elsie Burlen.

Lade came in about an hour later, and Stalley decided to have it out. "I asked Elsie Burlen to go to the dance with me, and she said she already had promised to go with you," Stalley said. "I didn't know you knew her well enough to ask her to go to a dance."

"And I didn't know you knew her well enough to ask her," Lade replied.

"Uh!" Stalley grunted. "Have we both been keeping something from the other?"

"Seems so," Lade said, grinning. "I didn't think that you'd be interested."

"Let's get to the bottom of this," Stalley begged. "We're getting along fine, Lade, and we don't want to make any mistakes. We don't want anything to happen that'll break up our friendship. Just how far have things gone with you and Elsie Burlen?"

"I've been seeing her regularly," Lade admitted. "And I guess that I—that I think a lot of her."

"Uh! And I've been seeing her regularly, too," Stalley said. "It's a peculiar thing, Lade. It seems that Elsie Burlen has been paying attention to nobody but us two. That's funny! Burlen has a pile, and we don't amount to much. If she had been giving all her time and attention to one of us, we could figure it a peculiar fascination, such as a woman undergoes now and then. But she wouldn't be infatuated with both of us at once, would she?"

"What do you mean, Stalley?"

"Elsie Burlen came home right after we refused to hook up with her father. Apparently she ignores everybody else and starts out to get you and me interested in her. Can't you read the answer, Lade? Two men in love with the same woman cannot be friends and partners, except under unusual circumstances."

"So she's been playing a game!"

"Unless I miss my guess, she has," Stalley said. "She never thought, I suppose, that we'd sit down and discuss the thing coolly, like this."

There was silence for a moment, while Lade looked out of the window and considered the situation. Then his face grew red, and he turned to face Stalley again. "That's it!" he said. "I've been a fool!"

"So have I," Stalley admitted. "When a fool knows he's been a fool he generally ceases to be one, Lade."

"I'm done!"

"Good! So am I. Burlen's daughter isn't strong enough to break up this combination, is she? Then we'll make a little agreement, Lade. We'll both avoid her. We'll not say anything to her about discovering her little game, but we'll stop playing in it."

Lade put out his hand, and Stalley took it. "So much for that!" Stalley said.

Both realized their narrow escape, and it had the effect of making them more careful in watching Burlen and his associates. Stalley saw that Burlen intended to wreck the partnership, and that he wanted to draw Stalley to his side if possible.

The partners were doing well, but they were compelled to be very careful now. They knew that Detective Michael Murphy had his eyes on them, was waiting for them to make a little slip. Murphy was not the sort of man to arrest them on suspicion. He wanted to get them when the evidence would be conclusive.

Both men ceased paying attention to Elsie Burlen, avoided her whenever it was possible, and, when they were forced to meet her, got away as soon as they could. Lade started it by pretending a sudden illness and getting out of acting as her escort to the dance.

Elsie Burlen sulked over it. She was not used to being ignored. Finally there came a day, after a night of serious thought, when she entered her father's office with a look of determination in her face. "I've failed!" she said. "They're wise. It's the only way I can account for it. I had both of them crazy about me, and all at once they began keeping out of my way. They compared notes, I suppose."

Burlen grew purple with wrath. "You must have made some silly mistake!" he said accusingly,

"I didn't! They're big friends, that's all. And now there's something else. You're always boasting, dad, that you can do as you please with people. You've told me a score of times that you could get me whatever I wanted."

"Well?" Burlen asked.

"The game has gone wrong," Elsie said. "It serves me right, I suppose. We never stopped to think that, in getting those two men infatuated with me, I might get infatuated with one of them."

"What?" Burlen roared.

"I've run around the country and seen everything," she went on. "And now I want to settle down and live as I should. I—I want a husband."

Burlen laughed. "There shouldn't be any trouble about that," he said. "There are hundreds of men who would marry Elsie Burlen, I guess. Besides being a girl whom any man could be proud to have, you've got a fortune coming when I'm done."

"Yes, there are hundreds," she said, "but there is a certain one I want."

"Who is he?"

"Stalley!" she said.

Burlen looked at her for a moment aghast, and then his anger broke. "Stalley!" he cried. "Why pick out that bull-headed donkey?"

"Make no mistake, dad, he isn't, a donkey. He's got more brains than you and all your friends. He's a man, even if he is a crook! He's not one of these boasting four-flushers. I want him, I say. He's the first man I ever met that I'd marry. The game didn't work, you see."

"You mean that you fell in love with Stalley?"

"I suppose so."

Burlen was thinking rapidly and presently smiled. "Well, it could be worse," he said. "It puts a sort of different complexion on matters, at that. I'll see Stalley."

He continued thinking after Elsie had gone. If Stalley were his son-in-law, Stalley naturally would hook up with Burlen. It would be to his advantage in every way. Burlen had not intended losing his daughter to gain an associate, but it would be better that way than no way at all.

He rang for Dan Clanner. "I want to see Stalley again," he said. "Get him here as quick as you can. Tell him that I don't want to talk about business, but something else to his advantage."

Dan Clanner went in search of his man, but the words of Burlen had made him think. Dan Clanner, since Elsie's return, had been unable to gain her favor, and he had noticed her preference for Stalley, had realized that she was interested in the man, beyond playing her father's game.

He found Stalley after a time and induced him to go to Burlen's office. He pretended to go away, but he did not. He went into a little room adjoining, where he could overhear the conversation.

Burlen greeted Stalley warmly, offered a cigar and sat chuckling for a momemt before he spoke. "You're going to give me the laugh when you hear what I've got to say, Stalley," he said finally. "But don't laugh too much. Just remember that I can't help it. If you were a father you'd understand."

"What are you driving at?" Stalley asked.

"Don't be in a hurry, this thing embarrasses me," said Burlen. "I'm going to come clean with you, Stalley. I told my girl to interest you and Lade, thinking that you'd get jealous and split, and then you'd either come in with me, or have to go it alone. Well, she tried, and I presume you men were wise enough to see the game."

"We were," Stalley said.

"And something happened. I hope, Stalley, that you learned to think something of Elsie, because she has fallen in love with you."

"What sort of a joke is this?" Stalley demanded, sitting up in his chair.

"It is no joke, Stalley, and no trick. My girl has fallen in love with you, and she wants you for her husband. Since you got wise to the game and have been avoiding her, she's been going around like a sick kitten. She confessed to me a couple of hours ago. It is no trick, Stalley. I want to see my girl happy."

Stalley made no reply. He was watching Burlen closely,

"I want you to understand," Burlen said. "Forget the trick we tried to play and make it up with the girl. She's a good girl, Stalley, and good to look at. And there'll be something coming to her when I'm gone, and something for her husband while I'm alive. Regarding our—er—business relations, you can continue having Lade for a partner. If you want to come in with me, all right. If you want to continue with Lade alone, all right. It's my girl I'm thinking of, not myself." Burlen thought he was safe in saying that. He knew that he could get Stalley, once Stalley was his son-in-law.

Stalley tossed away the remnant of his cigar, cleared his throat, and stood up.

"Then it's a deal?" Burlen asked. "You'll meet Elsie half way and not avoid her any more?"

"I am not interested," Stalley said.

"What's that? I tell you it is no trick, Stalley."

"And, in part, I believe you, Burlen. That isn't the idea. I am not interested in your daughter, I was for a few minutes, but I am not now."

"You're refusing to marry her, when she as good as asks you, through me."

"I have decided that I'll never marry, Burlen. But, were I to marry, it wouldn't be your daughter!"

Burlen sprang to his feet, rage in his face. "You refuse?" he asked.

"Absolutely!"

Burlen really did think a great deal of his daughter. Stalley's calm refusal of her made him a maniac for the time being. He shook his fist in Stalley's face. "Then I'll fix you!" he declared.

"I've handled bigger and better men than you, Stalley! You'll have cause to remember it! Get out of here!"

"I'm just going," Stalley replied.

CHAPTER VI
LADE WORKS SWIFTLY

IN the adjoining room, with his ear against the partition, Dan Clanner had heard it all. He kept quiet until the end of the interview, but he was storing up rage and wrath that would have to be expelled.

Stalley had scarcely reached the front door of the tobacco establishment, when Dan Clanner, without the courtesy of a knock, rushed into the office and confronted Burlen.

"So that's the game, is it?" he demanded* "I heard it, Burlen! I came in with you, and you said I could have Elsie some day. And she treats me like a dog, and you deliberately offer her to another man. What about me?"

"Why, she wouldn't look at you, you rat!" Burlen sneered. "Been listening, have you?"

"Yes. And I'm a rat, am I? Rat enough to do your dirty work for years and be your messenger boy! You remember that a rat can scrap when it's cornered! I know a few things about you, Burlen! And you'd toss me aside and get Stalley to be your right-hand man, if you could, would you?"

"Do you realize what you're saying, and who you're talking to?" Burlen demanded.

"You can bet your life I do!" Dan Clanner cried. "You've been playing me for an easy mark, have you? You won't play me for one any more, Burlen! You're not so high and mighty! Stalley and Lade don't seem to need you in their business; neither do I!"

"What's that?"

"You heard me, Burlen! I'm not going to be an easy mark any more. I'm done with you! And you just make a move, and see how far you get with it! I know a few things about you and your games, Burlen!"

"See here!"

"I'm done with the lot of you! Get somebody else to run your errands and do your dirty work! And you just try to make a move against me, just try it!"

He rushed from the office without another word, went into the street and hurried to the lodging house where he had a room, dashed up to the room and drank heavily of vile bootleg liquor which he had there. He was more than half afraid because of what he had said to Burlen, for he knew Burlen's power. But he had said it, and the words could not be recalled now. Dan Clanner decided that he would brazen it out.

After a time he went down into the street again. The cheap liquor had fanned the fire of his rage. He lurched into a pool hall, to find Stalley there, purchasing some cigars. Clanner thrust his way forward to Stalley's side. "Look here, Stalley," he said, "I heard what you and Burlen had to say about a certain girl. You stay out her way. Understand? If you don't, Stalley, you'll have me to deal with! You get me?"

Fifty men heard the words. Stalley, anger flooding his face, whirled and gripped Dan Clanner by the throat and shook him as a terrier shakes a rat.

"You rat!" Stalley exclaimed. "You dare to come in here and talk to me like that? Get away from me! If you act like this near me again, I'll choke the life out of you! Get out—and be quick about it!"

"I—" Clanner began.

"Get out, I said!" He hurled Dan Clanner from him with all his strength, and Clanner, muttering threats, went out into the street. Stalley bought his cigars and returned to his room to have a conference with Stubby Lade regarding something they had planned. Lade had been gathering information.

The news of the clash between Clanner and Stalley flashed through the district, and Burlen was one of the first to hear'it. He had told his daughter of his talk with Stalley and had seen anger flash in her eyes. Burlen sat before his desk and tried to think it out. Dan Clanner now was a real menace to him, for Clanner did know a lot that the district attorney would have given a great deal to know. And Burlen could not forgive Stalley for refusing his daughter. Here were two men it were best to remove.

Burlen had had men removed before and had suffered no qualms of conscience. It was nothing new for him. And so he sat before the desk and thought and planned and smoked one black cigar after another. After a time he sent for two thugs who were under obligations to him, and they talked in whispers and planned until long after the regular meal hour. Burlen passed them money, gave them careful instructions and sent them away.

The following morning he found that his daughter had not slept well. Her face was white, her eyes dark-rimmed. Burlen knew that she was suffering.

"I'll square it for you, Elsie!" he told her.

"You can't!" she said.

"Can't I? I've planned it already, girl. Refuse to marry you, will he? You'll have your revenge, all right. He's playing right into my hands."

"How do you mean?" she asked.

"You ought to know better than to ask me that. I'm not a man to go to talking wild about my plans, am I? Wait until it is over, and then I'll tell you just how I did it."

"Tell me now!" she said. "I'm as much interested as anybody. It's my right—"

"Possibly I'll tell you this evening," Burlen said, "but not now. I don't want anything to leak out accidentally, Elsie. But I'll square it for you with Stalley! Don't worry about that!"

She had to be contented with that, for Burlen hurried to his place of business without saying more. That day he received reports at intervals of every hour or so, and late in the afternoon he received the thugs again.

When evening came Burlen was acting peculiarly. His plans had been perfected, and he seemed to gloat over the fact. But there was a trace of nervousness in his manner, too. Even Burlen could not plan a double murder without flinching now and then at the thought of it.

"Tell me!" Elsie Burlen commanded, about nine o'clock, when she had her father alone.

"Why not wait until tomorrow?" Burlen asked.

"Because I'm interested in this."

"All right!" Burlen said. "Dan Clanner has kicked over the traces because he can't marry you. I was about to get rid of him, anyway. He's not the man he used to be. He heard me talking to Stalley and went wild."

"What about it?" she asked.

"Dan Clanner knows a lot, he knows too much. What generally happens to a man who knows too much about me?"

"I know," she said. "But I was thinking of Stalley, I didn't mean Dan Clanner."

"It's all in the same little game," Burlen told her. "Dan Clanner must be got out of the way. It's necessary, if I am to be safe. And Stalley, the man who turned up his nose at you and has openly flouted me, he ought to be got out of the way, too."

"How?" she demanded.

"Stalley and Clanner had a scene, a scrap over you. That's the way it looks to the mob. Fifty men heard Stalley threaten to kill Clanner, if Dan again accosted him. Well, if Clanner is found dead, and Stalley can't show a good alibi."

Burlen ceased speaking. Elsie's face went white again, and she clasped her hands nervously. "I see," she said. "Some of your thugs are to kill Clanner, and Stalley will be accused of the crime."

"Precisely," Burlen said. "That's enough, now! But, when Stalley is in prison, waiting for his execution, you'll know what he is suffering, and then you'll have your revenge! Just forget all about it now."

"But I want to know more," she said, "Who is to do the work? And how are you sure that it'll be fixed on Stalley?"

"Leave such things to me," her father said sternly. "I've told you too much already. But you were so hurt about Stalley refusing, that I thought I'd let you know your revenge was planned."

"Don't do it!" she begged. "We'll find some other way."

"It happens to be too late. It'll be done in about an hour," Burlen told her. "The men who are to do it have Clanner with them now. They're leading him to the slaughter, the rat! Threaten me, will he?"

"You might be implicated," she said.

"Trust me to plan well," her father replied. "I am not worrying about myself."

"But I wish you'd tell me more!"

"All right!" he said angrily. "I'll tell you more, and then you'll shut up and leave me alone. Stalley is a gambler, and he is in a card game this minute. He'll stay there, too, for he'll be winning. Understand? My men will keep him if he tries to go away.

"While he is there, playing cards, Dan Clanner will be killed. Everything will point to Stalley. The cops will find him in the card game. He'll say that he has been playing there all evening. And my friends will declare that he stepped into the room and got in the game less than half an hour before."

"Oh!" she gasped. "They'll swear his life away!"

Burlen looked up in amazement at the expression in her face. "Are you still in love with the fool?" Burlen asked. "Want to protect him after he's curled up his nose at the thought of marrying you? He thinks he's somebody, compared to you!"

"But I am afraid for you," she said. "If it ever comes out and the police learn that you framed it—"

"It'll not come out!" Burlen told her. "That's enough, now. Run away and let me alone."

"I hope there'll be no slip," she said, "Where is Stalley playing cards?"

"I've told you enough, and I'll tell you no more," Burlen said. "Run away!"

Elsie Burlen hurried from her father's room and went to her own. There she listened and waited until she had heard her father leave for the tobacco establishment. Then she dressed for the street.

Burlen had made a mistake. Elsie had not been moping because of Stalley's insult in refusing her. She had been acting peculiarly because she really loved Stalley, and she realized that she had lost him by playing her father's game. And now she found herself in a terrible predicament. She wanted to save Stalley, but she did not want to injure her father. And her father must never know that she had saved Stalley, either. She would have saved Clanner, too, despite the fact that he was a menace to Burlen, but she knew there was no chance for that. Less than an hour, her father had said, and half that time had passed.

She hurried out into the street and went to the lodging house where Stalley and Lade lived. She asked for Stalley and found, as she had feared, that he was not at home. Then she asked for Lade, and it happened that he was in. Lade had contracted a cold and was keeping close to his room.

The girl had to whisper her intelligence to Lade, because there were other persons near. She knew from the look in Lade's face that he would do all he could, but that he was afraid, too.

"I don't know where he's playin' cards," Lade said. "He plays in a lot of different places. Chances are, I couldn't find him under an hour."

"You got to find him, got to save him," she declared. "And you must save my father, too. You've given me your word!"

"I wish I hadn't," Lade declared. "It'd be simple, then, I could tell my story to the cops, and they'd grab everything and everybody."

"You've got to do something!" she said again.

"You go home and leave it to me!" Lade said.

Elsie Burlen hurried back to the street, and Lade went to his room and put on his coat and hat. Never in his life had he thought as swiftly as he did now. He knew Burlen's power, though he scoffed at it. He guessed that there was no way out for Stalley. If he denounced Burlen, despite his promise to Elsie, he would not be believed. The police would think that Stalley had done the murder anyway, possibly at Burlen's orders. Burlen might be caused some trouble, but that would not save Stalley.

And Lade had little time in which to act. He dared not try to find Stalley, for there were a hundred places where a quiet game of cards might be in progress, and he had scant time. And then the solution came to him, and, though the first thought of it was terrible, Lade saw that it was the only way. He hurried down into the street, like the Lade of old, filled with fear, lacking confidence, gulping, his hands twitching nervously.

"They've made a plant for Stalley," he told himself. "Stalley made something of me. He saved me once. Now I've got to save him. It's a plant, and it's got to fail!"

He had his chance, then, to do as many men would have done. He could have remained in his room, to let Stalley take his chances. He could have protected himself easily. But he thought of nothing except Stalley, the man who once had saved him, the man who had been his friend.

The idea had flashed into his head, and he knew that it was good. He decided to use it, though it would cost both Stalley and himself a great deal. He hurried to a drug store on a corner, went into a telephone booth and called police headquarters. He asked for Detective Mike Murphy. Lade was fortunate, for Murphy was there, having been called in to identify a man wanted elsewhere. "Listen!" said Lade in a hoarse voice. "Two men have just robbed Berstein's jewelry store. They double-crossed me, too. I think you'd like to land 'em. Get hold of Stalley or Stubby Lade, as quick as you can, and maybe you'll catch 'em with the goods!"

Hanging up the receiver he left the busy drug store, quite sure that nobody had recognized him. He hurried two blocks up the street to Berstein's jewelry store. It was an establishment that he and Stalley had marked for robbery, but it was to have come some time in the future, when all plans had been completed.

Lade hurried around into the dark alley. He was careful that nobody saw him. At the rear of the jewelry store he worked lor a time at a basement window. Ten minutes later he was in the store proper. He gave the big vault no attention. But, under the counter, there was a fireproof box that Lade opened swiftly. He filled his coat pockets with diamond rings, taken from the box.

Out into the alley he hurried again, and, on his way, he left a plain trail. He reached the street and sauntered along it. He had not gone more than three blocks before his shoulder was grasped, and he whirled around to see Detective Michael Murphy.

"What's the idea?" Lade asked.

"Where have you been for the last hour or so?" Murphy demanded.

"Oh, just around!"

"Uh-huh!" Murphy slammed him back against a wall and began exploring. He found the diamond rings.

"Been around, have you?" he asked. "Around Berstein's jewelry store, I guess. We'll check up the place for fingerprints and things later. Wise man, are you? You and your partner?

Not so very wise! I expected something better than this from you. Where's Stalley?"

"Stalley? I haven't seen him since early this afternoon," said Lade.

"No? I suppose not! He wasn't with you, eh? Better come clean with me, Lade. You're small fry, a sort of servant for Stalley. I want Stalley. You come clean and help me and I'll see that the judge goes light with you."

Lade gulped and looked down at his feet. "I—I—" he stammered slowly.

"Was Stalley with you when you robbed that store?" Detective Murphy demanded.

"Yes!" Lade said.

"Ah! And where is he?"

"I don't know."

"Got swag on him?"

"No. I carried all that. We couldn't get into the safe, you see."

"You come along with me!" Murphy commanded.

Stubby Lade, for the first time in his life, felt handcuffs on his fat wrists. He gulped again and went along with the detective. They passed other officers, and Michael Murphy mentioned the man whom he was after. He questioned stool pigeons, too, and crooks of the. district. Finally he got a straight tip. Stalley, his informant said, was playing cards in a certain back room, in the rear of a well-known pool hall.

CHAPTER VII
LADE'S TRICK

TAKING Lade with him, Murphy proceeded to the pool hall. He kicked open the door of the rear room and strode inside, pulling Lade after him. Five men were playing cards, and Stalley was one of them. They sprang to their feet, and Stalley looked in surprise at Lade and the handcuffs. "Careful!" Detective Murphy warned. "This isn't a raid on a card game. Stalley, how long have you been here?"

"Since about six in the evening," Stalley said. "Why?"

"All the time?"

"Yes."

"Haven't left the room?"

"I haven't."

"Stalley, you're a liar!"

"Ask the boys," Stalley said.

"All right, I'm asking them" Detective Murphy glared around the room, and waited.

"I don't know what this is all about," spoke up one of Burlen's hirelings, "so I suppose we better tell the truth."

"You'd better!" said Murphy,

"All right. Stalley came in here about half an hour ago,"

"Hadn't been here before tonight?"

"No, sir."

"Ah, ha!" Detective Murphy gloated. "What have you to say to that, Stalley?"

"It's a lie!" Stalley declared. "I've been here since six o'clock. Ask the others!"

Murphy asked, and they all said that Stalley had come in within the half hour.

"Lies!" Stalley reiterated. "This is some sort of a plant."

"I guess not," said Murphy. "You're my prisoner, Stalley, so don't try any fancy tricks. You and Lade robbed Berstein's jewelry store a short time ago. I caught Lade with his pockets full of diamonds."

"It's a lie!" Stalley repeated. "I don't know anything about the jewelry store!"

"No use running a bluff, Stalley," Murphy said. "I've got you this time. Lade admits that you were with him."

"Lade—" Stalley stopped, and his eyes met Lade's squarely. Lade was begging him mutely to acknowledge the charge. But Stalley did not understand. He and Lade had been planning to rob that store, and now he thought that Lade had tried it alone so he could take all the profit.

And Lade, on top of that, it seemed, had said that Stalley had been along. After all Stalley had done for him, after the friends they had been! There was another element, too. These men, Burlen's men, had lied about him being in the room. Stalley saw that it was a trap. And he remembered that he had been invited to this game.

Was Lade, after all, a Burlen man? Had he turned against Stalley because of Elsie Burlen?

"Lade, you ungrateful dog!" Stalley said in a low voice.

Lade begged him again with his eyes, but Stalley did not look at him after that one remark.

"So you admit it, do you?" Murphy asked.

"No! I wasn't near Berstein's," Stalley declared. "This is a trap, I say! Maybe you'll get me, but I'll stick by what I say. I wasn't near that jewelry store. I have been right here, in this room, since six o'clock, playing cards."

"Uh-huh!" Murphy replied. "You heard what these four men said, didn't you? They said you came half an hour ago. Come along with me, Stalley,"

He hooked Stalley to Lade, and Stalley deliberately turned his face away from that of the other man. Murphy took them out to the street corner and rang for the patrol.

"You cur!" Stalley whispered to Lade.

"Stalley, I—"

"Don't talk to me!"

"I want to explain."

"I don't want to listen!" Stalley said. "Murphy, I wish you'd take this skunk as far as possible from me!"

"Oh, you'll have different cells," Detective Murphy said.

THEY WERE separated at the jail, and Stalley went into his cell to sit on the bunk and marvel at the ingratitude of mankind. Lade, in his own cell, felt Stalley's hate and hoped that soon he would know the truth.

Stalley did not sleep that night. He tried to figure it out. At first he thought that Lade had attempted a trick alone and so had been caught. But he remembered how the men in the card room had lied. That meant that Burlen had a hand in the game. "He's thrown me down and joined Burlen and helped frame me," he told himself. "Or else he's turned stool pigeon and is working for Murphy. They'll let him off, I suppose, and hand it to me! But, when I get out, he'll get his."

This was the first time he had been arrested. Even if they convicted him, the sentence would be light.

MORNING came, and with it Detective Murphy and another officer. They took Stalley from his cell and conducted him to a room where attorneys interviewed their clients. Murphy disappeared and, when he returned, brought Lade with him.

"I don't want to be in the same room with that rat!" Stalley said.

"Suppose you try to control yourself, Stalley," Murphy said. "I can imagine what you are feeling. I understand that you have been friends with Lade. I know about the Burlen girl. Lade hasn't thrown you down, Stalley. I'd say that Lade was pretty much of a man."

"You might think so," Stalley sneered.

"Suppose you and Lade listen to me. Last night, Dan Clanner was knifed. Two of Burlen's thugs did it because Clanner had quit Burlen and he knew too much. But it happened that a couple of plain-clothes men, drifting around town, looking for a suspect, stumbled onto the party. They caught the murderers red-handed. They confessed and implicated Burlen.

They had been ordered to put Dan Clanner out of the way and fix the crime on you, Stalley!"

"What?" Stalley gasped.

"Exactly! You were playing cards with Burlen's friends. They were to swear, as they did, that you had been there only half an hour. Everything was fixed for you to be suspected of the murder. A knife belonging to you was used. Your recent quarrel with Dan Clanner over a woman furnished the motive. It was a neat plant, Stalley, and it promised to succeed. It was an accident that the two plain-clothes men happened by."

"Then Lade—"

"Lade was loyal enough to save you, Stalley. I suppose it did look bad, but he was really doing you a favor. Elsie Burlen loved you, you see, and she hurried to Lade and told him the plot. Lade couldn't find you in time, and so—I'm guessing at a part of this, but Lade can tell us if it is correct—and so he did his best to save you, anyway.

"He robbed that jewelry store, Stalley. He did it crudely, as you'd realize if you looked it over. He left clues purposely, including a handkerchief with your laundry mark. Somebody telephoned me to pick Lade up, and when I did, he had his pockets stuffed with diamonds. Lade, did you telephone?"

"Yes," Lade replied.

"And then, Stalley, Lade told me that you had been with him. Do you understand? If you had been with Lade robbing that jewelry store, you couldn't have been killing Dan Clanner, two thirds of a mile away. Lade framed it on the spur of the moment to get you four or five years in prison instead of the electric chair. Understand, Stalley?"

"Lade!" Stalley cried, "Forgive me, Lade!"

"It's all right, Stalley," Lade said. "We've been pals."

"And there you are!" Detective Murphy declared. "We know, now, that you didn't rob the jewelry store, Stalley. So you're free to get out of here."

"But, Lade?" Stalley questioned.

"He did rob the store, you see, and must go up for trial. But I think a lot of a man, even a crook, who'd do such a thing. I'll explain to the judge, and Lade undoubtedly will help the State in the trial of Burlen. I think it is safe to say that Lade will get off with a light sentence. We recovered all the diamonds, you see."

Stalley got up slowly and crossed to Lade, and Detective Michael Murphy did not try to stop him, no matter what the regulations might say.

"Lade!" Stalley said. He held out his hand, and Lade grasped it. "I—I'm glad to know that I hadn't made a mistake about you, Lade. You see, you're the first real pal I ever had. I'll do what I can for you, Lade. I'll stand by you! And when you get out, Lade, I'll be waiting at the gate!"

"That's all right, Stalley!"

"If I can do anything for you—"

"You might make sure," said Lade, "that I have plenty of cigarettes."

"I'm sorry for what I said last night, Lade."

"It's all right, Stalley! I suppose it did look bad."

Detective Murphy cleared his throat by way of warning.

"Stalley," Lade said, "I'd—I'd say a word or two to Elsie, if I were you. She's square, that girl—and strong for you, Stalley! She did her best to save you."

"I'll see her," Stalley said.

He gripped Lade's hand again, and then Lade was led back to his cell. But Lade was smiling. Things were all right again between him and Stalley. That was enough to satisfy him.

www.ingramcontent.com/pod-product-compliance
Lightning Source LLC
Chambersburg PA
CBHW030541180626
46810CB00005B/1961